# HOUSE OF GLASS HEARTS

MW00882971

LEILA
SIDDIQUI

HOUSE
OF
GLASS
HEARTS

YALI BOOKS
NEW YORK

Published by Yali Books, New York

Text © 2021 by Leila Siddiqui
Cover Art by Aishwarya Sadasivan

Connect with us online: yalibooks.com
Instagram / Twitter / Facebook: @yalibooks
Pinterest: @yali_books

All rights reserved. No part of this book may be reproduced or transmitted
in any form or by any means, electronic or mechanical, including
photocopying, recording, or by any information storage and retrieval
system, without the written permission of the publisher.

Library of Congress Control Number: 2021933942

ISBN: 978-1-949528-77-0

978-1-949528-78-7 (Hardcover)
978-1-949528-76-3 (eBook)

Typeset in Adobe Garamond Pro and Smoothy

*To my grandparents and their collective histories*

# PROLOGUE

Karachi, Pakistan, 2011

Asad tossed and turned in bed, jet lag leaving him unable to sleep for yet another night. He lay on the roof of his naana's house, wrestling with the sheet that had enveloped him as he roiled in bed. Asad kicked it away and sat up, wiping the sweat from his brow. He sighed as a cool breeze trickled past him.

For the hundredth time that summer, Asad wished his best friend were with him, seeing the same sights, smelling the same smells, eating the same foods, and going on brazen adventures with him. Asad imagined Bobby back in Virginia, eating breakfast at his table with his family, missing him too. Not for the first time that summer, Asad truly felt alone. The only kids his age were his cousins, and barely any of them spoke English. His little sister, Maera, was too young and constantly attached to Ammi's hip to play. And Ammi was always squabbling with her sister or Naana to pay him any mind.

"I wish you were here," Asad whispered, hoping the wind would carry his words across the planet to Bobby.

He glanced around at the still sleeping forms of his cousins scattered across the roof. They'd made their beds up there because the bedrooms had become too hot and stuffy to sleep in, and their parents had kept shouting at them to quit tossing and turning so loudly. Once freed from their parents, they could chatter and play games late into the night until the cooled evening air lulled them to sleep.

Maera slept serenely beside Asad, her hands tucked under her pillow. He pulled the sheet up to cover her, then kissed her on her forehead.

"Sweet dreams," he said and smiled, sure that his voice had made its way into her dreams. "I'll be right back."

He crawled off the mattress and stretched his arms over his head. The stars winked down at him, and he winked back. Something else caught his eye, glimmering in the darkness. Asad heard a series of creaks and groans and turned to the back of the house where the greenhouse lived.

The backyard was where Naana never allowed the kids to go. They had the run of the house, but the backyard was off-limits, barricaded by a heavy wooden door. Asad had had his ears twisted and cheeks pinched hard by his aunts and Ammi for fiddling with it, and gotten a severe scolding from Naana for even walking past it. Tonight, Asad was done following the rules.

A pale green light emanated from the greenhouse, visible from the rooftop. It seemed to pulse to the rhythm of Asad's heartbeat. He thought of Bobby again. He knew that if his friend could read his mind at that very moment, he'd understand how terribly bored Asad had been all summer and would egg him on from afar to spring into a new adventure.

Asad dug under his pillow for the toys Baba had lovingly carved for him—little zoo animals he could never bear to part with. Baba had told him these were his "tokens of courage". Asad held them in one palm, inhaled the dry wood smell of them, and then stuffed them into his pocket.

Maera stirred and rolled over to his side, blinking the sleep out of her eyes. "Are you trying to get in trouble or something?"

Asad grinned at her. "Maybe I am."

On the mattress beside him, his younger cousin Jamal sat up, rubbing his eyes. "Where are you going?" he asked, his voice heavy with sleep.

"Just on one of my adventures. You both better not think about following me. Go back to sleep."

Asad weaved between the cots and made his way to the stairs. He peeked back at Maera and Jamal, both sitting up and glaring at him. He gave them a small wave and headed down the steps to Naana's courtyard.

A dark shape appeared to be seated on Naana's takht. Asad gasped and flattened himself against the wall. A thin cloud passed over the moon, and the shape disappeared.

Asad crept up to the cracked wooden door that led to the backyard. He imagined an eerie forest of gnarled black trees beyond, blanketed by fog like in a dark fairy tale, and the forbidden greenhouse brimming with untold treasures. Tonight, he was going to find out what his naana kept hidden from all of them.

The backyard wasn't a creepy forest: it was carpeted with springy grass and bordered by hedges that grew close to a high wall surrounding the backyard. Clumps of trees stood at the back with their heads conspiratorially close. It would have been as ordinary as Asad's backyard at home, except for the giant greenhouse that sat in the middle.

It was waiting for him. A dim green light pulsed from the center, and a murky wind swirled inside. Asad dug into his pockets and clutched his tokens of courage in both palms.

A cold sweat trickled down his back and made him shiver. He gave the door handle a light shake, cringing at the metallic clang it made. He gave it another tug, but the door wouldn't budge. Asad turned back to the roof, trying to think up another way to get in until a creaking noise made him jump.

He stepped up to the door. "Who's in there?" he asked, his voice just above a whisper.

The greenhouse groaned in response. And then, the door opened on its own, just a sliver but large enough for Asad to fit through. He tapped the glass, and it wobbled at his touch. Asad took a deep breath and passed through the door. He was immediately bathed in green light. He gasped, and the toys fell from his hands. As he crawled on the ground to pick them up, a long shadow fell upon him. He shaded his eyes from the light and blinked up at the figure standing before him.

As the sun rose that morning, Maera shook herself awake from a terrible nightmare. She'd been in a forest, running after Asad for miles and miles, but the faster she ran, the further away he was. She awoke out of breath, as if she'd never stopped running.

She reached for her big brother, but the space beside her was empty. Then she heard the frantic shouts from her various family members downstairs.

As the shouts grew louder, the other kids got up and crawled over to the edge of the roof to look down into Naana's courtyard. Her cousin Jamal was awake, his eyes large and afraid as he rolled over to one side. They exchanged glances, but Jamal looked away. He covered his face with his hands.

Their naana's house was being searched, ransacked, the doors of neighbors were being pounded on, taxis were being flagged down in the middle of the street—their neighborhood a tumult of shouts and cries and the pounding of feet on baked earth. Maera and her cousins stayed up on the roof through mid-day, stomachs growling and foreheads baking in the sun, unable to move, terrified that if they joined the others, they'd only get in the way.

When the children finally made their way off the roof and down into the bowels of the house, Maera heard Ammi wail, muffled by what she imagined were Baba's arms. A pit of grief opened up inside her. She didn't know it then, but for the next ten years, she'd carry that raw, gaping wound within her.

Asad was gone, and he was never coming back.

# ONE

# THE GREENHOUSE

On the first day of summer break and the morning after her grandfather died, it appeared in Maera's backyard. It was a hulking mess of wrought iron and plates of glass, a green-tinged monstrosity that thrust upward into the air.

Maera pressed her nose against the window and watched it quiver in the sunlight, bathed in orange beams. She pushed her glasses up to her forehead and rubbed her eyes, but when her glasses slid back into place, the specter didn't disappear. Her breath fogged against the window as she watched the structure stretch and shift in the morning light, then settle into a permanent repose.

Maera backed away from the window, a scream lodged in her throat as the curtains rustled. It gleamed into her room beyond the curtains, spilling bright light through the cracks and throwing reflections against the walls. Maera reached for the phone under her pillow, but her hand ran over a grimy object instead. She shrieked and threw her pillow aside.

She found an old diary covered in cracked brown leather, its edges frayed and yellow. The book was bound by a leather strap and fastened at the end by a tiny lock. Maera's temples throbbed as she frantically looked for her phone and found it wedged between the bed and wall. She pressed the home button, but the dead battery symbol flashed across the screen.

"Ammi!" she called out. Usually, the kitchen was rife with the sounds and the smells of breakfast. Ammi was a noisy, messy cook. But this morning, the house was silent. Maera ran downstairs to Ammi's bedroom and almost threw open the door when she heard a sob and a discreet sniff into a tissue.

Maera knocked on the door. "There's something strange going on," she said. "Something really weird. I'm kind of scared."

Ammi opened the door in a white shalwar kameez, a soft white dupatta over her head. Her beautiful eyes were red with tears, but they'd been like that for years now.

"What's happened?" Ammi asked and touched Maera's face, leaving a damp handprint on her cheek.

Maera cringed and waited for her mother to turn away so she could wipe her face on her sleeve. "There's a creepy thing in our backyard."

Ammi hurried into the kitchen and stared out of the window. Maera plugged her phone into the charger. She set it down on the table with shaking hands, waiting to hear it buzz to life so she could immediately call the police or Sara or somebody about the alien in her backyard.

Ammi turned to Maera. A green halo formed around her as her head and shoulders blocked the view from the window.

"There's nothing out there," she declared. She moved away to the fridge, and as she did, the thing outside came into view and nearly blinded Maera.

"Right there!" Maera exclaimed, pointing outside. "You don't see that?"

Ammi cracked eggs into a bowl and whisked them. The fork made jagged clinks against the ceramic sides. "See what, beta?"

"That thing." Panic bubbled up Maera's chest. "You really don't see it, do you." It wasn't a question anymore. Ammi appeared not to hear her as she scraped at a pan, cooking an omelet for the two of them.

"I'm dreaming," Maera said. "This is a nightmare. I'm an unwilling participant in an elaborate nightmare."

A beam of tremulous light entered through the kitchen window. The structure appeared unchanged, but this time Maera spotted something she hadn't seen before. Her phone buzzed twice, but she ignored it and stepped up to the window above the sink.

It wasn't any ordinary building. It was a greenhouse with long glass walls and a sloping roof. At the center of its facade was a door.

"What the hell is going on?" Maera squinted to see inside, but the panes were sooty and covered in something green.

"Hmmm?" Ammi asked, pouring milk into a pot of chai.

"It appeared out of nowhere this morning," Maera replied. A cloud drifted past the sun, and the greenhouse winked at her.

"That's impossible," Ammi said. "It's always been there."

"It hasn't. It showed up overnight, right after we found out about Naana—"

Ammi looked puzzled. "What are you talking about?"

From the tone Ammi took, Maera knew it wasn't really a question. Just like always, like their entire history together, The Past remained in The Past. Deaths and disappearances were pushed back there. Heartache and heartbreak were packed away and sent on a one-way journey to The Past.

Maera ran back up the stairs to her room. The diary lay undisturbed on her pillow. She picked up the old thing to sniff the pages. They smelled of iron, and the dust tickled her nose. But there was something else too—a powerful odor of melancholy that made her want to hug the book to her chest and comfort it in some way. Maera felt a tingle in her fingertips and, along with it, the profound sorrow that came with finding something old and forgotten. She carried it down to the kitchen and thrust it into Ammi's hands.

"That thing outside appeared this morning, and this notebook showed up in my room," she said. "None of this is normal."

Ammi's eyes were wide as she gazed at the diary. It looked even sadder in her trembling hands.

"Where did you get this?" she asked. She turned it over and over, running her fingers along the cracks.

"I told you—it randomly showed up," Maera said, hugging herself. "I don't know what's going on, but I'm really scared right now."

Just like Maera, Ammi brought the notebook up to her nose and sniffed. She frowned. "This was his diary." She clutched it in her hands, her knuckles bone-white against the leather. Ammi pulled on the lock, but it didn't come loose.

She picked at the corners to reveal the edge of a page scrawled with dark curly handwriting. They leaned in together to make out the words.

The greenhouse creaked outside. Maera stared out of the window, watching the structure breathe in and out, quivering in the warm air. Ammi began to say something, but a low hiss distracted her. The pot of chai bubbled over on the stove, angry flames underneath flickering blue and orange. Ammi tsk-tsked under her breath and turned the knob to lower the flame.

"Why don't you believe me?" Maera asked.

Ammi hugged the notebook to her chest. "Where did you get this?"

"I told you," Maera said, hands on her hips. "It showed up. Like that thing outside." It was one of the many things Ammi refused to see, but Maera couldn't find herself to say the words.

The diary left a smudge of grime against Ammi's chest, but Ammi didn't notice. She chewed the inside of her mouth. For a moment, Maera thought she saw a spark in her eyes, a realization that something strange was going on.

"My chacha mailed it," Ammi said. She looked down at the diary. "I need you to tell me when you check the mail."

"Did your uncle also mail *that*?" Maera jabbed a finger at the window. "Can you please just tell me what's going on?"

Ammi rubbed her forehead and sighed. "Your naana said he was leaving us something after he passed. He never told me what it was." It was a rare acknowledgment of The Past, an allusion to a past conversation.

Maera took a breath. "What was he going to leave you?"

"A part of his house. He had a big house." Glassy-eyed, Ammi stared off at some distant memory. "Me and your khala would chase each other from room to room. When I think about it now, it felt like a palace, so much larger than it actually was." Ammi blinked a few times, then she was back in The Present, back to the notebook in her hands. She plopped it down onto the counter. "I guess this was all he left me. Wash up, and I'll have breakfast ready."

Maera waited for more from her mother, but the conversation was decidedly over. She unplugged her phone and ran up to her room. There was a flurry of good-morning texts from Sara, the happy "last summer till we're seniors" texts. Rather than respond, she pulled aside the curtain and glared out at the greenhouse, now awash in sunlight. It looked like a giant gemstone reflecting light in all directions. Maera stepped back to take a picture of the greenhouse, blocking the glare with her hands. The only image that appeared on her phone was a turquoise sunburst. She texted it to Sara with a note: *am I going crazy or was this thing always here?*

Sara responded right away: *did you and your mom finally have your talk?*

Maera took another picture of the greenhouse, but again it only showed up as a bright ball of light. Her phone buzzed. Another text from Sara: *i'm coming over.*

Maera headed back downstairs and poked her head into the kitchen. The notebook was still sitting on the counter. Ammi picked it up and turned it over in her hands again.

"I think I'll go lie down for a while," she whispered. She slipped past Maera, taking the book with her.

Maera stared at the greenhouse through the kitchen window. Its glassy green eye stared back. The way the sun shone on the greenhouse, it looked like it had caught fire, with geometric flames engulfing the structure.

Her phone buzzed, and she flinched. "Stupid," she said to herself. Another message from Sara: *here.*

Maera unlocked the front door and, before Sara could step in, threw her arms around Sara's shoulders, bringing Sara down to her height. "I really, really need you right now."

Sara laughed and struggled out of her grasp, though with her long limbs, it was easy to escape Maera. Her hair was balayaged and highlighted, ready for summer before Maera was.

Maera led Sara into the kitchen. "Did you see the pictures I sent you?"

Sara didn't hear her as she scanned the table. Ammi had laid out breakfast for them—her version of scrambled eggs with onion, jalapeños, and cilantro, sprinkled with chaat masala, with pan-toasted sandwich bread. Sara tore up pieces of toast and scooped egg into her mouth.

Maera noticed Ammi's mug of chai sat untouched on the counter. It was still hot; wisps of steam trailed upward and disappeared into the air.

Maera hovered over Sara. "Did you see the pics or not?"

"Hey," Sara broke up more pieces of toast, "did you guys finally talk?"

"There's something strange going on," Maera said. She lowered her voice. "Ever since my naana died . . ."

"What?" Sara looked up at Maera with her impossibly large eyes. "Your naana passed away?"

"Yes, he did, but—"

"When?"

"We found out last night."

"Why didn't you tell me?" Sara asked with genuine hurt in her voice.

Maera ran a hand through her short bob. "I guess it was a big deal over there, but not a big deal in this house." Maera imagined her eyes watering, a visible lump forming in her throat. Something to show the world that she wasn't an unfeeling robot, that she was distraught at Naana's passing. But there was absolutely nothing.

Her grandfather had quietly passed, and she couldn't even manage a tear.

"It's a big deal. Your mom's dad passed away." Sara sounded shocked. She turned to call Ammi, but Maera shushed her.

"We've got bigger problems. Look outside."

Sara followed her gaze to the window. Her face morphed into a question. "That wasn't here on Saturday."

"It was my naana's. It was in his backyard. In Pakistan."

Sara's eyes went wide as she grappled with her back pocket for her phone. She swiped to the pictures Maera had sent and then looked back up at the greenhouse. "How did it get here?"

"Like I would know. My mom thinks it's been here all along. She won't even notice it. It showed up this morning out of nowhere. It looked like it was building itself." Sara stared out of the window.

She whispered, "Why is it here?"

"I think my naana has something to do with it."

"You're scaring me." Sara rubbed the goosebumps on her arms. "Past-tense, deceased Naana or like present-tense, maybe-not-really-deceased Naana?"

Maera glared at the greenhouse. "Like present-tense Naana."

TWO

# THE MEMORY

They stood barefoot in the grass and stared up at the beast. The late morning heat was heavy around their shoulders.

"I changed my mind," Sara said. "Let's go back inside and investigate from there."

Maera touched her hand. "If we're doing this thing, we're doing it together."

Sara squeezed Maera's hand and they approached the structure together. It seemed to swell the closer they came. The air around the greenhouse hummed like a hive of invisible bees.

Maera placed her hands on the ground to feel the vibrations. The grass trembled in the direction of the greenhouse.

"It's like we're on a plane or a spaceship," Maera said.

They stepped closer, and the buzzing entered Maera's feet, traveling up her torso to her teeth. Her fillings clattered, and she clutched her head.

"None of this feels right," Sara said. Her skin turned sallow. "I feel sick. Can we go inside?"

The air around them stilled. The sounds of summer returned, leaves whispering in the trees and squirrels crashing among the branches.

"It stopped. That was weird." Maera rubbed her jaw where her molars still ached. She moved to one end of the greenhouse's facade. "Okay, I'll go down this way, and you go down the other side."

Sara wouldn't move. "Are we sure about this?"

"We need to find out what this thing is." Maera peered down the edge of the greenhouse. Behind her, Sara disappeared around the other side. The walls spanned the length of the backyard, the smooth plates of glass reflecting lazy clouds swirling by. She reached for the glass and touched a finger to it. It exuded a human warmth from within. Maera waited for something to happen, and when it didn't, placed her whole palm against it.

A faint drumbeat pulsed against her skin. She whipped her hand away and ran to the end, when Sara emerged from the other side.

"What are we thinking?" Sara asked, tapping a finger to her chin. "Twenty by thirty?"

Maera wrung her hands, the strange warmth of the glass still on her skin. "It could be much bigger than that." They were behind the structure now, and it looked the same all the way around.

Sara grabbed Maera's arm. "There's movement in there."

They stepped closer to the glass, squinting at the murky, swampy light inside. Maera made out the shape of large fronds. They bent back of their own will, then waved at her. Maera sucked in her breath.

"Something's definitely in there," Maera whispered, moving closer to the glass until her nose was almost touching it.

The fronds swayed again. "There must be some sort of ecosystem in there."

Sara held up her phone to record a video. Maera peeked over her shoulder as the lens adjusted itself. They stared through the phone, but life inside the greenhouse stilled. Sara tapped on her phone several times. "I keep pressing record. Nothing happens."

"Because this thing in my backyard is otherworldly."

They made their way back around and stood before the door. The handle was rusty, gleaming wetly from the morning dew. Maera flexed her hand. Then, she gripped the handle and pulled it down. It caught and clicked.

"Locked." Maera wiped her hand on her pajama bottoms, leaving a streak of rust along her thigh. She stood staring up at the top of the greenhouse when she felt a tug on her arm.

"Come on. I don't like this. Let's not upset the thing."

They headed back to the patio and into the kitchen, where Ammi sat at the table, cupping her chai in her hands. Sara squealed and hugged her.

When Sara pulled away and sat down next to her, Ammi moved Sara's hair off her shoulder and gave her a pleasant smile. "You've gotten so tall. Just like your brother."

"I'm taller than him now. I'm definitely taller." Sara smiled at Ammi. Once again, Maera was left out of their conversation, standing by uselessly while they chattered on.

"He's in college still?" Ammi asked.

"In Texas, where I'm thinking of applying."

Ammi sat back in surprise. "Your mother allowed it?"

Sara glanced at Maera. A blush crept up Sara's neck.

"It's—we figured it out. He'll be there to chaperone us. I mean me."

"Okay, are we going to just forget about that thing that is outside? That it's possibly alive?" Maera asked. "Are you guys even listening to me right now?"

Ammi turned to Maera and gave her a once-over. "We have guests coming tomorrow. No full-day PJs, okay?"

"I like full-day PJs," Maera said, crossing her arms.

Ammi wrapped her long fingers around her cup again. "Your khala and Jamal are on their way to the airport."

Maera put a hand to her forehead and brushed aside the strands plastered to her face. "Wow, so I'm living in a nightmare, and we have guests coming." She looked to Sara for help, but Sara went on eating the food Ammi had warmed for them.

"I don't remember you telling me." Maera stared at her mother.

Sara stopped eating and wiped her mouth with a napkin. "I'll go wait in your room," she said and left the kitchen, floorboards creaking as she made her way up the stairs.

They eyed each other for a moment, then Maera let the pressure release from her shoulders and slumped down into the seat across from Ammi.

"I'm sorry. I'm being difficult as usual." What Maera wanted to tell her was that she hated seeing her ammi in a constant state of sorrow and that she wished she'd have the power to make everything better again. That someday their broken family would be whole. But she couldn't bring herself to say the words.

Ammi slid her hand over and held Maera's. "I know it's not easy losing someone."

Maera stared up at the ceiling and resisted the urge to roll her eyes. "But I didn't know him."

"Sometimes, I feel like I didn't know him either. But a loss is a loss."

Maera glanced out at the greenhouse and felt her mother watching her.

"How long are they here for?"

Ammi withdrew her hand and went back to contemplating her chai. "Just until the will is sorted. We can't drop everything and run to Pakistan." Ammi sighed and ran a hand through her hair. Wisps of gray surfaced then disappeared among her dark tresses.

An intimate look of pain passed over Ammi's face. "And I said I'd never go back."

Maera waited for more, but her mother sat tight-lipped, clutching her cooled tea as if it were the only thing anchoring her to the world.

Back in her room, Maera planted herself at the window and gazed out at the monster. It stared back at her, unflinching and unmoving. Behind her, Sara hugged a pillow to her chest. "I'm sorry about your naana."

"Did you know yours?" Maera asked, turning her back to the window, the heat of the greenhouse's eye on her back. "Did you know your grandparents?"

Sara plucked at the edges of the pillow. "Not really. We talk on the phone and send pictures to each other. But I don't *know* know them."

"Don't you think it's weird that we don't have what other people have?" Maera asked.

Sara shook her head. "We're brown. We'll never have what other people have, especially with their grandparents. I mean, we were born here, and they continued to live there. Mine don't even speak English. It's a struggle talking to them, and you know I have horrible Urdu."

Maera looked down at her feet. "Sometimes, I wish I saw more of my grandparents. That I had a real relationship with them."

"Okay," Sarah moved the pillow aside, "what's really going on?"

Maera studied the four corners of her room. "Maybe if I had a normal family and it wasn't just me and my mom all the time, I wouldn't be so desperate to leave. Did you see what happened downstairs?"

Sara shrugged. "Maybe she's not ready to talk about it with you."

"But she was talking with you. She hasn't asked me once where I'm planning on applying. It's like if she brings it up, it'll give me the idea to run away." Maera sat next to Sara and drew her legs up, hugging her knees to her chest. "And now this thing appears outside. Like an omen."

"No. Not these 'signs' and 'omens' again."

Maera glanced at the window.

"Last night, after we found out about my naana, it was the same old doom and gloom from her. I came up here and sent a panicky email to an advisor to visit in the fall."

"Without telling me?"

Maera shrugged. "Seeing the way my mom was last night made me impatient."

"When you tell her, it'll be all right. She'll understand."

Maera had a sudden urge to tear her curtains aside and scream at the thing outside. "It'll be her usual reaction. Lots of tears and then shutting herself up in her room." Maera rested her chin on her knees. "That's why I wish I had a whole family."

"You have me. And your mom," Sara said in a small voice. For a moment, silence filled the gap between them. It was a while before Sara spoke again. "I get it. But I'm not your mom. Talk to me."

Maera pressed her lips together, the kind of reaction she usually had with Ammi, physically shutting herself up before she'd say something to hurt her. But Sara eyed her expectantly, leaned forward a little as she waited for her to speak.

Maera sighed. "For some reason, he feels closer now more than ever. This used to be his room."

Sara smiled. "You never told me that before."

"He had Spider-Man posters all over the walls. He was obsessed with superheroes. So annoying." Maera laughed.

"I wish I knew him. I wish we'd met a little earlier."

Maera grinned at the thought. "You would have loved him. He'd be like the big brother you wish you had."

"I already have two. I don't need any more than that." Sara wrinkled her nose.

Maera glanced back at the behemoth outside. "Ever since this greenhouse appeared, I can't stop thinking about him."

"I can't either," Sara whispered. "It's almost as if he's right here, right here in this room with us. And I never even met him."

"You're lucky you're not stuck with the same memories on loop. Replaying them over and over again." Maera breathed out, allowed the old scars she'd bandaged away years ago to reopen like ugly wounds. "I keep thinking I'd do something different, but it's always the same. Always the morning Asad went missing. We thought he was hiding in the backyard. That's where this thing stood. I still remember how scared I was of it, how enormous and old and terrifying it was." Maera hadn't realized she was crying. She wiped her tears on her sleeve. "And how easy it was for someone like Asad to sneak into, especially when we weren't allowed to go near it. He could get into anything."

Sara stared out of the window. "It's here now. You're not forbidden from it anymore."

Maera sniffed, letting the tears trickle down the sides of her face and into her hair. The sensation wasn't entirely unpleasant. It was as if she were making up for the years she'd spent bottling her tears in the first place.

"I think my naana's trying to tell me something. He's sent it to me for a reason."

Sara let out a low whistle. "We brown people are so haunted."

## THREE

# THE VISITORS

Sara and Maera spent the night the only way they knew how. They snuggled under the blanket and pretended to be asleep so Sara's mother wouldn't have the heart to wake her and drag her away, tripping and clumsy with sleep. While the girls lay in bed, their mothers whispered outside the door. Ammi peered in for a moment, and the girls stilled their bodies, stifling their giggles until their mothers left them alone and their footsteps creaked down the stairs.

"All clear," Maera whispered. She imagined Ammi slinking back to her bedroom for another lonely, tearful night.

As if she'd read her mind, Sara burrowed closer to Maera. "It's going to be okay." She threw a lazy arm over Maera. "Tomorrow's a new day."

"And we can figure out how to get rid of the thing outside?" Maera yawned, but Sara had already drifted off to sleep.

Outside her window, the greenhouse shone silver against the rising moon. Framed by the pearly light shimmering through the curtains, a face appeared at the window.

It was Asad, looking like he did the night he went missing.

Maera sat up and blinked. She slipped her glasses on, but before her eyes could adjust to the dim light, the face was gone.

Sara slept unaware as Maera settled back into bed and pulled the blanket over her head. It was a while before she managed to fall asleep.

Maera awoke to the sounds of the front door opening and shutting, followed by strange voices in her house. It was morning, and she had somehow slept the whole night without waking. Next to her, Sara slept with her mouth open, tiny snores gurgling out of the depths of her mouth. Maera rubbed the sleep from her eyes and reached under her pillow for her glasses, but something else was in its place.

The notebook had returned, undisturbed. Her glasses were squeezed against the wall. "How did you get back here?"

Sara stirred next to her. "What?"

"Nothing. Go back to sleep," Maera whispered.

Sara rolled over and mumbled in her sleep. For a moment, Maera hoped she'd dreamed up the diary's appearance, that the greenhouse returned to where it belonged, and that life had gone back to normal, whatever their definition of normal meant. But when Maera tumbled out of bed and pulled the curtains aside, there it was, looking as if it always belonged there. It stared at her with full force. Maera scowled back at it and headed out of the room.

Ammi and Aisha Khala stood at the front door facing one another, the differences between them still striking. Though they were twins, Ammi was a frail wisp compared to her sister.

Aisha Khala wore a tight white blouse and high-waisted flared trousers, also white. Her wrists clacked with white bangles and her hair came down in soft waves. She was resplendent as always, while Ammi looked sad and shrunken next to her.

They sensed Maera on the stairs and turned at the same time, smiling the same smile.

"Look at my baby girl!" Aisha Khala pulled Maera into a hug, bangles clattering. Buried in Aisha Khala's chest, Maera found that she smelled like a woman of the world.

Aisha Khala held Maera out at arm's length. "You're just as perfect as I remembered."

Maera felt her face grow hot under Aisha Khala's stare. Over her shoulder, she could see Ammi standing back with clasped hands, the white dupatta from the day before framing her face.

The front door opened, and her cousin walked in, struggling with the luggage. After ten years, she'd forgotten what he looked like. Now, as he managed to pull his suitcase into the foyer and extend his hand to Maera, she saw the resemblance to their mothers. The same long face and small inquisitive eyes, highlighted by his short-cropped hair.

"Hi."

Maera barely heard him. It was as if he didn't say the words so much as he breathed them out.

Maera shook his clammy hand. "Hi, Jamal."

"Jimmy," said Jamal and Aisha Khala together. Aisha Khala tittered. "We can be Americans too, just like you." She tapped Maera on the nose.

"Aisha," Ammi said, her mouth set in a tight line.

"I'm joking. We can't forget our sense of humor, can we? The old fool dies, and we forget how to laugh."

Maera and Ammi shared a surprised glance. Behind them, the stairs creaked. Sara stood on the steps, frozen in mid-flight, staring back and forth at the mothers.

"My God, there's two of them!"

Aisha Khala and Jimmy gave Maera questioning looks.

"This is my best friend, Sara," Maera explained. "She lives down the street."

"So cute," Aisha Khala purred.

"Maera, chai. Please," Ammi said in a tremulous voice. Then she reached for Aisha Khala and Jimmy, keeping them at arm's length. "I'll show you where you'll be sleeping."

Sara followed Maera into the kitchen. "I thought your mom was gorgeous, but your aunt is just sexy."

Maera placed a pot of water on the stove. "They were always different like that. My mom's more of the earth, and Aisha Khala is more . . . not."

"Glamorous." Sara outlined the shape of a very generous hourglass with her hands. "Curvaceous. I mean, stunning. Where has she been all my life?"

"Far from us." Maera turned the knob to high. "Writing her Pakistani dramas."

"Ugh, she's so amazing," Sara said. "Does she write all the racy ones? The dramas that, like, 'imply' sex, but don't show it?"

Maera shrugged and busied herself looking for teabags. Her aunt's provocations had grown old with her and Ammi.

"Hey." Sara looked at her.

"Did you look out the window?" Maera asked. "It's still there. I woke up this morning and thought I'd dreamed it all. It's still there. Have you forgotten?"

Sara looked out of the kitchen window. "I haven't. I haven't at all."

The water simmered and hissed up the sides of the pot. Maera threw in six teabags and watched the water swirl around them and pull them under the surface. "So why are you pretending like everything's okay?"

"I guess I didn't think about it first thing this morning." Sara shrugged. "I've adapted to its appearance. It's harmless."

"Harmless? It showed up out of nowhere. And now it's tricking us into thinking it's been there all along."

Sara looked puzzled for a moment. Maera pushed herself back onto the counter, as far back as she could get from Sara. "You thought that, didn't you? It tricked you."

Sara shook her head. "I can't imagine what you're going through right now. Why don't I finish making the chai, and you can catch up with your family."

"I can do it myself," Maera protested, but Sara was already at the stove, blocking her from the bubbling pot.

"Go. And tell your cousin I said 'hi.'"

Maera raised an eyebrow, but Sara had turned her back. She headed up to the guest room. Inside, Ammi and Aisha Khala were whispering in feverish, urgent tones. Maera put her ear to the crack in the door, but they were so artfully quiet, she couldn't make out their words.

"They'll be at it for a while," Jimmy said from behind her in crisp, accented English.

Maera jumped and placed a hand over her thumping heart. "Do you always sneak up on people? You scared me."

Jimmy leaned against the wall. "I'm sorry about our loss."

It took Maera a second to remember. "Oh, right. Sad about our naana too. Were you guys close?"

"My mother wanted there to be as much distance as possible between us without having to leave the country. That's why we moved to Lahore."

"I thought it was for her, um, entertainment career?"

"There were other reasons." He glanced at Maera's room and pointed with his chin. "That used to be Asad's room."

"You remember." Maera stepped closer to him. He nodded.

"I still remember your house. The last time I was here, Asad was here. For a second there, I thought I saw him in your room." Jimmy laughed to himself. "Probably jet lag."

"Then I must be having jet lag too." Maera moved closer to Jimmy so the mothers wouldn't hear. "Last night, I thought I saw him in my room."

Jimmy raised an eyebrow. "Is this a joke?"

"I need to show you something." Maera led him into her room. She parted the curtains and waited till Jimmy blinked to make out the shape outside. "Look familiar?"

Beside her, Jimmy stiffened and gripped the window sill. "It's the same. Impossible."

As they watched, the greenhouse appeared to bristle under their stares. The facade groaned, and the handle jerked downward of its own accord. They leaned forward, their breaths fogging the glass.

The door swung open. Inside, fronds rustled, and a dirt path appeared through the murky fog. Jimmy turned to her, questions flickering across his face.

A knock on the door startled them, but it was only Sara. She hugged herself.

"Hi." She looked at Jimmy, and then her eyes widened as she looked past them at the behemoth outside—at its open, inviting door.

"Still think it's harmless?" Maera asked. Sara joined them at the window as the door swung in the wind.

"We have to go in there." Maera gripped Sara's arm, giving it a vicious shake. "Now." She pulled Sara to the door, but Jimmy stopped them.

"You shouldn't. It could be dangerous."

Maera eyed him. "Do you know something we don't?"

"It could be dangerous," he repeated. "We don't know anything about it."

"That door was locked yesterday. Now it's open, and this could be our only chance. We don't know how long it's going to stay open."

"You're talking about it like it's a living thing," Sara said. "It's just a . . . a building."

"It's not just a building," Maera pushed past them and ran down the stairs. Ammi and Aisha Khala sat at the table in the kitchen. Maera tried to make her way to the patio door, but Khala stood up and blocked her path.

"There you are."

Jimmy and Sara appeared behind Maera in the kitchen.

"We were thinking," Aisha Khala added, with a shifty glance at Ammi, who was staring at a spot beyond her sister, "that we should go out like a mod-run family and have breakfast somewhere. Leave the house for a little bit."

Ammi cleared her throat. "We have to pray."

"For a little bit." Aisha Khala smiled. "We'll spend the rest of the day praying after."

Maera glanced at the kitchen window. The door stood open, the dirt path leading to some unimaginable place.

"Can I just catch up with my cousin?" Maera asked. "Show him around the backyard, you know, hang out outside?"

The mothers exchanged glances, and then Ammi said, "It might be good for us all to get out for some fresh air."

When Maera looked back at the greenhouse, its door was shut.

# FOUR

# THE BOY NEXT DOOR

Sara protested and protested, but Ammi sent her home, citing her mother's concerns that she'd barely seen her daughter since summer began. Maera walked Sara outside and watched her sprint down the road on her long legs, turn the corner and vanish into their neighborhood.

Maera then headed to the car where Ammi was already in the driver's seat, gripping the steering wheel. Maera slipped into the passenger seat and touched her mother's arm. Ammi blinked a few times to reorient herself.

"You're so good," Ammi said. "You're good for indulging me." She stared ahead at the road. "Sometimes those four walls close in on us."

Outside, Aisha Khala tapped the driver's side window. She had bright red lipstick splashed on her lips; she bent down. "We're ready," she said in a sing-song voice.

Once the seat belts clicked, and the four of them settled into their seats, Ammi drove them into Old Town Alexandria and pulled up to an unassuming diner. Ammi hadn't bothered to change out of her white shalwar kameez, as if mourning the dead meant wrapping yourself in white for as long as possible.

Maera and Jimmy were in jeans and T-shirts, and Aisha Khala had on a glamorous white dress. They trooped in after Ammi and waited behind her as she asked for a table in perfect English. The hostess gave Ammi a once-over and smiled a tad too much. "Right this way, ma'am," she said and led them to a cozy booth next to a window.

Aisha Khala made little approving sounds, cooing at their surroundings and the pretty view from their booth. "I always love coming to America. It makes me very popular with my friends, doesn't it?" She nudged Jimmy, and he nodded, though he stared at the table. Aisha Khala poked him again. "They must be talking about me right now, wondering what I'm doing."

"Or maybe they're praying for your loss," Ammi said, her gaze fixed on her sister. The waitress arrived with a painted smile, perhaps sensing the tension between the two beautiful, similar-looking brown women at the table.

She listed the specials, but Aisha Khala stopped her with a raised hand. "Look, I don't know anything about a Benedict or a Madame or a Mansoor. We want eggs, honey. And toast and coffee." The rest of them murmured their orders, and the waitress scribbled it down.

"Was I rude?" Aisha Khala asked when the waitress left.

"You were you." Jimmy smiled.

Aisha Khala grinned at his response, then trained her smoky eyes on Maera and Ammi. She cupped Maera's chin in her hands. "Just look at my baby girl. Look how big you are. You're going to college soon?"

Ammi stiffened beside her, but Maera stared straight ahead at Aisha Khala. "I guess I am."

Ammi sighed and moved to the end of the booth. "I need to wash my hands."

Aisha Khala eyed her as she slid out and, when she was safely out of sight, leaned her ample bosom toward Maera. "She's probably going in there to cry. How are you handling his death?"

Maera shrugged. "Fine. We're fine."

"It's okay not to be upset. He was a bitter old man. He was never nice to his daughters. Treated us like we were abominations."

Jimmy fidgeted in the seat next to his mother.

"Oh, right. Naana's the reason she's upset," Maera said, wondering if her aunt was as aware of Ammi's mercurial nature.

Aisha Khala had an intriguing smirk on her face. She was such an open book, shamelessly provocative when it came to their family's secrets, and Maera found the invitation to unbury Ammi's past all too enticing.

"Why was he so terrible anyways?" Maera asked. She wanted to remember him but was unable to conjure up any memories of him. The only image she had of him was of an old man with pink cheeks and a bushy white beard from the one picture Ammi had of him, which she kept on the mantle above the fireplace. It was a rare smile, a mysterious happy moment for him, and Ammi never explained the photograph.

Aisha Khala sat back against the booth, hands in her lap. "He was in the war. The bad one."

Maera's mouth hung open in surprise. She glanced at Jimmy. "Which war? You can't mean—"

"Second World War," Aisha Khala said. Beside her, Jimmy's eyes grew wide.

"World War II?" Maera asked. "He fought in World War II?"

"He didn't fight in the war. He tried to follow his own abbu to the front line. It was traumatic for him."

"Wait. Wait. My great-grandfather fought in World War II? I thought it was just the British. And like, Europe and America?"

"Aren't they teaching you proper history in your schools?" Aisha Khala shook her head sadly. She turned to Jimmy. "Did you learn proper history?"

"Not much about the war," he admitted.

Maera gripped the seat underneath her to steady herself. She hadn't expected the revelations to be so startling, especially the appalling realization that the heroism and glory she'd learned about had never been about her brown ancestors. India's part in the war was reduced to a tiny blip, a footnote in her history classes. In books and movies and everything she'd ever known, the big wars were fought between good white guys and their white enemies. It was a bunch of Tom Hanks and Hardys fighting courageously, martyred as heroes, while countless brown experiences were stripped from those narratives. Now a piece of that history was hers, and she had no idea what to do with it, even as she realized that it never belonged to her anyways.

But something had changed. Her whole existence now had an undercurrent of importance she never thought was possible.

"I can't believe I never thought to ask."

"It isn't your fault if your own people don't want to talk about it. It wasn't our war, after all," Aisha Khala said. "You think we want to be reminded of that?"

"I obviously wouldn't know." Maera sat back and crossed her arms. "Is that why Naana was so . . . odd?"

"He never told us much about his past." Aisha Khala crumpled a napkin in her hand. "Hid it away much as your ammi does. We never knew much, just the little things our uncles told us." Aisha Khala scoffed at the memory of him. "He was such an unhappy old man. He had very high standards. Like when Amna ran off to marry your father."

Maera felt her heart squeeze in her chest. When it came to talking about The Past, Ammi's usual response was to retract her head like a turtle into the protective shell she had created for them. But the woman in front of her was different, so worldly and comfortable dredging everything up. Maera found herself leaning toward her aunt, pulled to her by her illicit sharing of secrets.

"I'm not allowed to talk about my abbu," Maera said, grief crawling up her throat and lodging itself there no matter how much she tried to swallow. "It's as if he never existed. It's as if Asad never existed either."

"I'm sorry, beta. I don't agree with pretending our hearts never broke. If it makes you feel better, your naana didn't approve of my late husband either, for that matter." Aisha Khala had a faraway smile on her face. "Of all the women, you'd think I'd be the one with the runaway husband."

She winked at Maera, and Maera glimpsed the cracks in her facade. A break in her cheerful voice. The wrinkles around Aisha Khala's eyes from the many sleepless nights spent sending tearful pleas to God. The tremor in her chin. The thin wedding band she still wore on her finger.

"If you ever need someone to talk to, we're here for you," Aisha Khala said.

Ammi appeared suddenly next to Maera, sniffling back tears as she slid into the booth. She pointed her chin at her sister, her twin sense somehow aware that Aisha Khala had divulged too much to her daughter.

Their food arrived. Maera and Ammi took a shared vow of silence while Aisha Khala talked on without interruption. She brought up the weather in Lahore, the Pakistani elections, the serial she was working on ("A young widow opens a beauty salon in Jackson Heights and falls in love with a married Bengali man. Then she marries his son!"). Ammi slid her eggs around her plate and answered in grunts and nods while Jimmy spent most of the time staring out of the window.

Once home, Maera headed straight for the patio, but Aisha Khala was already in the kitchen, standing in her way. "Your mother wants us to pray for our father."

"I really need to go outside to, um, get some fresh air."

Aisha Khala smiled and ruffled Maera's bob. "Go do this for her, please?"

Maera glanced at the green monster outside. "I'll pray next time around."

Aisha Khala put her hands on Maera's shoulders and gently turned her around. "Just for a little while. Off you go."

Maera sighed. She headed up to her room and put on a pair of shalwar kameez. She wrapped a dupatta around her head and dug out the Quran her dad had bought her two years ago, before he walked out of the house for the last time. It had been that long since she'd last read it.

She took the Quran down with her and settled with the mothers on the sofa in the living room, propped up by pillows and cushions. They fell into their respective Qurans in silence—Maera's in English, Aisha Khala's translated in Urdu, and Ammi's in the old Arabic. Upstairs in the guest room, Jimmy sat on the bed with his Urdu translation.

Maera read without reading, her mind wandering to the greenhouse outside—how the setting sun might be reflecting off its edges, casting pretty shapes on the ground. Beside her, Aisha Khala read fast, licking her finger as she flicked through the pages. Ammi stared at her book, her eyes navigating around the old cursive, caressing each ligature, sounding the words out under her breath until she turned the next page.

Maera cleared her throat. "Can I take a break?"

Ammi glanced up, her finger planted on the page where she'd been interrupted. Before she could respond, Aisha Khala cut in. "Let her take a break. This puts me to sleep sometimes, too," she said with a giggle. Ammi sighed through her nose and shook her head, but Aisha Khala went on, "I can read for her. I was always the faster one anyways."

Ammi looked back down at her page. "That's because you cheat and skim the page."

"You're released," Aisha Khala declared. Maera didn't wait for her mother's permission. She placed the Quran in Aisha Khala's outstretched palm and slipped into the kitchen. She studied the greenhouse through the window. The waning sunlight moved along its edges and gave it an ethereal glow.

Maera waited, tapping her fingers on the kitchen counter. The living room behind her was silent except for the occasional flick of a page and a deep-throated sigh. She unwrapped the dupatta from her head, dropped it on the counter, and headed for the patio door. She turned the lock as softly as she could. It scraped against the wood as springs and tumblers shifted around and made a tiny click, but not loud enough for Ammi to hear. Maera pushed the door inch by inch, her hands trembling from keeping it as quiet as possible until it was wide enough to let her through. She shut it with a soft whomp behind her.

It was fast approaching sunset, and a cold sliver of wind, an unusual holdover from spring, snaked itself around her. Maera rubbed the goosebumps on her arms and approached the greenhouse. It glowed with a murky, swampy light from within.

Maera placed her hand against the glass. It was soft and warm, and it pulsed under her skin, more alive than the last time she touched it. She peeked inside, pressing her forehead against the glass. She followed the trail as far as it would go before it was completely engulfed by green.

At the very end of the trail, a thin figure emerged with its arms to its side. Maera sucked in her breath, but she couldn't blink or look away as it turned its head in her direction. The figure was tall, a fully-grown person.

"It can't be."

The whine of creaking wood made Maera jump back from the greenhouse. She glanced at the fence where someone had pushed three planks outward toward her backyard from the other side. A night breeze blew against her as she listened to the tell-tale crunch of footsteps on the grass. Maera turned back to the greenhouse, but the figure had disappeared.

Bobby Marquez, dressed in sweatpants slung low, and a faded Georgetown T-shirt, strode into view. He stared at the greenhouse in front of them, arms crossed over his broad chest. He seemed unaware of Maera, who staggered back at the sudden appearance of a familiar yet unfamiliar boy. A lifetime had passed since she'd last spoken to him, and she struggled to reconcile the dim memories she had with the grown boy in front of her, someone who jogged past her house on the odd morning run. When she'd see him, she'd turn away and busy herself with something else.

But now he was in front of her, approaching the greenhouse. Bobby shuddered and pitched forward. Maera ran to him to take hold of his arm and was momentarily taken aback by the soft warmth of his skin.

"You can see it. You can see it too."

Bobby flinched at her touch and stumbled back. "Jesus Christ, you scared me." Tiny dots of sweat crowded on his forehead; a couple took over his upper lip.

"What just happened to me?"

Maera stepped back and crossed her arms. "I don't know what you're talking about."

"Really." Bobby wiped the sweat from his forehead with the back of a hand. "You said 'you can see it too.'"

"What are you doing in my backyard, Bobby?" Maera asked in a soft voice. It had been ten years since Asad went missing and exactly ten years since she'd last seen Bobby. She flinched at her memory of him from the day of the funeral. Maera had buried that day so deep that when it surfaced, she could taste the last thing she ate that morning, smell the gouged earth on the backs of the tires as they'd left the cemetery, and feel the hopelessness she felt when they'd arrived back at their somber, mirthless house. Then, when his parents had come to pay their respects, she'd caught a glimpse of Bobby in the doorway being his usual forlorn self, unable to meet anyone's eyes, unable to speak a word.

At the sound of his name, Bobby flushed. "I go by Rob now," he said. "In ten years, no one's called me Bobby, not since . . . I'm sorry. I didn't mean to bring anything up."

Maera uncrossed her arms and let them drop to her sides. "You didn't answer my question."

Rob stared back at her. Those inky black eyes of his made Maera feel young and small again. "I don't know why, but I felt like I needed to be here right now."

The greenhouse eyed them as Maera moved closer to Rob. "You've been thinking about him."

"I dreamed about him," Rob said. He rubbed his arms and shivered so slightly that Maera felt it more than she saw it. "I know it sounds weird. Especially after all these years."

"Trust me. You're not the only one."

"It's been so long, you think you forget and then . . ." Rob chewed on his bottom lip.

The greenhouse glowered next to them, but Maera paid it no mind. "Tell me about your dream," she said, her voice barely above a whisper.

He stared up at the greenhouse. "Asad was trapped in this place, in this jungle. He was afraid, but he also wasn't afraid. He felt like he was lost and he'd never come back, but that he was okay never coming back. Then I woke up," Rob touched his cheek. Maera wasn't sure if he was wiping a tear or touching his skin to remind himself that he was awake now, back in his own body. He withdrew his hand. "I woke up, and I thought this was the closest I'd ever been to my best friend."

"I had a dream too, about the night that Asad went missing," Maera said. "This might sound insane, and you're probably not going to believe me, but I think this greenhouse has something to do with it."

"It's just an ugly old building."

"It also sprouted up overnight."

Rob stepped back with a look of disbelief. "That's not possible."

"I knew you wouldn't believe me." Maera pushed her glasses up the bridge of her nose. "With the way my week's been going, anything's possible at this point."

A sound disturbed the night air: a thick, hollow clang of something being hurled at the glass. They gasped and moved away from the greenhouse.

"It came from inside." Maera left Rob's side and approached the greenhouse door.

"Don't," Rob whispered, but Maera had wrapped her fingers around the handle.

She took a breath, counted to three, and pushed the handle down. Still locked. She jiggled the handle and pulled on it with all her strength. When it didn't budge, she pounded against the glass door.

Rob moved close to her. She felt the warmth from his chest radiating along her spine as he drew her away. "I don't trust it," he said. "Maybe we should leave it alone."

"This thing here," Maera protested, "this thing that only we see as strange and unusual has brought Asad back up to the surface. It's opened the floodgates for everyone I know, including you. I've spent years forced to forget what happened to him, to pretend like he never existed. And then this thing—" She slapped the front door. "This thing appears, and he's all we can think about."

The wind blew them closer to each other, their bodies unconsciously seeking each other for warmth. Rob breathed deeply next to her. She watched the gentle rise and fall of his chest straining through his T-shirt and was glad it was too dark for Rob to catch her staring.

"You may have been forced to forget, but I wasn't," Rob said with a clenched jaw. "I had to grieve alone because your whole family shut me out."

"I didn't know." Maera lied. He'd looked so lost when Maera's parents met his family at the door. The moment before Ammi shut the door on them, for the briefest of moments, they'd made eye contact. He was never let back into the house again.

"I guess it's too late to say sorry." Maera touched his arm, her fingers lingering against his warm skin.

But Rob went on, "One minute he goes to Pakistan with you and the next you all return minus my best friend."

Maera winced. He'd brought up The Past so naturally, not the way she kept it close to her like a dirty secret, filling her aura like a dust cloud.

"We couldn't tell anyone because no one would understand. He just disappeared."

Rob turned away from the greenhouse and back to Maera. "In school, they said—"

"I know what we said. He had disappeared in a way in which we knew he couldn't return. He was as good as dead." Maera fell silent, shocked by how bitter the words were once she'd said them aloud.

Rob rubbed the back of his neck. "I never forgot him. I never wanted to."

"I wish I did." Maera placed a hand over her heart. She hadn't meant to say the words, but there they were, out in the open, simmering in the air between her and Rob. His mouth formed a surprised O.

Behind them, the patio door slid open. Maera stepped away, creating distance between them as Aisha Khala walked across to where they stood, crunching the grass underfoot. In the dark, Maera couldn't make out the look on her aunt's face.

"What are you doing out here?" Aisha Khala asked in a sing-song voice. She raised an appraising eyebrow in Rob's direction. "And who is this boy?"

"Our neighbor," Maera responded before Rob could introduce himself. "He was Asad's friend in elementary school."

"How sweet." Aisha Khala glanced at the two of them.

"And we were investigating how this thing appeared out of nowhere," Maera added, still watching her aunt. Aisha Khala cocked her head to one side and considered the monster in their midst. She then turned her gaze back to Maera and Rob.

"Come inside. It's my night to make dinner for all my babies."

Without a second glance at the greenhouse, she turned on her heel and headed back in through the patio door.

"Did you see that?" Maera asked. "For some reason, none of the adults realize it's shown up out of nowhere."

"Technically, I'm an adult. I'm nineteen."

"But you knew Asad. You two were like brothers. I think you have that connection to him." Maera stepped back from Rob, and though it pained her, she turned away from him. "I have to go."

"Wait." Rob took two long strides to catch up with her. "I want to help."

Maera eyed him. He stood with his hands in his pockets; the moonlight streaked his hair. She was so focused on how his presence had startled her that she hadn't given herself the chance to reconcile her memories of him as a boy with the person in front of her. That long-ago idea she had of Bobby was gone. That quiet boy Asad used to play with, who'd lower his gaze when he walked, fold his arms into his body as if his long limbs were an inconvenience to the world, his footsteps so light that Maera often thought he hovered over the earth rather than walked on it. That Bobby was gone, replaced with this newer, more alluring version. His posture now was assertive and strong; his legs planted firmly on the ground. It took her only seconds to take him in, and she was struck by the thought that maybe Asad's disappearance allowed the boy from The Past to grow into this new person.

Maera looked away, a slight blush creeping up her cheeks. "Meet me back here in three hours," she said and walked away, leaving him standing at the front of the greenhouse.

Maera ducked into the kitchen, where pots and pans bubbled on the stove. The whole place smelled like biryani masala.

"I don't need your help." Aisha Khala shooed Ammi away with a bangled hand.

"Oh, stop," Ammi said, stirring a pot of rice.

"I can help." Maera was relieved when the mothers didn't hear her. She slipped out of the kitchen and into the living room, where Jimmy lay on the couch. He had finished his reading.

"That was fast."

Jimmy stared up at the ceiling. "It's faster reading it in my language."

"Your language?" Maera exclaimed. "Of course." She ran past him and bounded up the stairs. The diary was no longer on her pillow. She dug under her blanket, tossing it into a giant ball, but it was nowhere to be found.

Maera fell to her knees and searched under her bed. There, the familiar rectangular shape of the diary was buried under a cloud of dust, like it had been there for years, untouched. Maera pulled it out and blew the dust off. Her fingers tingled again as she hugged it close to her chest. Then, heart thumping against the leather, she brought it down to Jimmy. Their mothers were making a grand amount of noise in the kitchen, clinking pans and bickering away.

Maera held it out to him. "If you pull at that top corner there, you might be able to make out a few words."

Jimmy sat up and held the diary in his hands. He did the same thing Maera had done when she'd first laid eyes on it. He ran his finger across the cracks, and considered each groove, each bump. He turned it over and over.

"My hands feel weird," he said.

"That happened to me, too."

Jimmy brought the lock closer to his face. "Wow," he said. "Very interesting."

"Try to pull it open there." Maera pointed at the corner.

Jimmy touched the thin leather cord around his neck, something Maera had seen him wearing since he'd arrived. The end disappeared into his clothes. He pulled it out of his shirt and then slipped the necklace off. At the end of the leather cord was a tiny gold key bound in a knot.

"Where did you get that?"

"It was given to me by our naana on my birthday. He mailed it in a small package with no note inside. I'd wondered why," Jimmy said, contemplating the key in the palm of his hand. "The size looks right."

Maera glanced at the kitchen. "I don't know how much time we have."

The key slipped into the lock with a satisfying click. It snapped open. Jimmy unraveled the thick leather strap around the diary and peeled open the first page. Bits of paper and cracked leather fluttered into his lap.

Maera hissed, "Be careful."

Jimmy ran a hand over the cover page where Maera made out a few haphazard lines in Urdu. She raised a hand to her glasses and pushed them further up her nose, trying to concentrate on the words, but they made no sense. Jimmy flipped through a few pages, his eyes scanning the lines. Finally, he stopped and placed a finger on a page, tracing the words from right to left.

"Oh. Wow."

Jimmy looked up at her with blank eyes, like he'd awoken from a dream. "This is his diary. A summary of his life."

"So Naana wrote a memoir. What does it say about that thing outside?"

Jimmy's eyelashes fluttered as he flipped through the pages. Maera wished she was inside his mind, reading the cramped letters that curled along the page just beyond her comprehension.

"Maera and Jimmy," Aisha Khala called from the kitchen, "can you come in and help us?"

Jimmy continued rifling through the pages until Maera put a hand on his arm. He looked up with a far-off gaze.

"We have been summoned."

Jimmy stared at the diary in his hands until Maera plucked it away and closed the book. She rewound the leather cord, hesitated for a second, then locked it.

"We need to read it," Jimmy said, his eyes hungry for more.

"We don't have the time right now. Let's get dinner over with, and regroup after to figure this thing out."

Jimmy nodded with a forlorn look. Maera slipped the diary under a couch cushion, leaving him sulking on the couch.

# FIVE

# THE WAR

Cawnpore, India, 1941

*Once upon a time, there was a boy and a girl.*
*But before they met, there was a war.*

Now that I begin to commit my memories into this diary, it feels like a hundred years have passed between when the entire world was at war and now. A war between good men and bad; a jang that propelled its way into the country and my life; a jang to end all jangs.

I sat on the floor in our old house in Cawnpore—a house I'll probably never see again in my lifetime—and watched my big brothers wrestle with each other at the table.

Ammi stood to the side, a cup of chai gripped in her hands while Papa sat at the table across from them. As my brothers tousled with each other, Papa threw his arm out to separate them. "All of my sons," he said, "all of them are crazy."

I made a noise of protest, but no one heard me.

Moosa put Yusuf into a headlock, and they laughed the same laugh. "I'll be the king of the sky," Moosa said. "Not you."

Yusuf untangled himself. "You wait until we're back in Jodhpur. I'll show you who the real king is. No one can dive like me," he said. He made a sweeping motion with his hand and let out a long trilling whistle.

"What's it like when you're in the sky?" I asked.

The twins turned to me as if they'd just remembered I was in the room. "Come here," Moosa said. He put an arm around me and drew me in closer. "Imagine," he said. He waved his hand across an empty sky. "You can see everything. The ends of the desert. The mountains. You can fly into the clouds!"

"How do the clouds feel?" I asked.

"Wet and windy and miserable." Yusuf chuckled.

"You feel like a god," Moosa went on. "And suddenly, this world feels very small."

"And the war?" I asked, screwing my eyes shut to imagine it all. "Can you see it yet?"

"It's only you and the sky and the world beneath you. It's peaceful enough to make you forget who you are and where you came from."

I opened my eyes and smiled up at Ammi. "Then I will join the Air Force too," I said. "Please?"

Ammi's smile faltered. She stared at her chai.

Yusuf chucked me under the chin. "Another ten years, baba, when you're an old man like us."

Moosa tickled me, and I yelped and wrenched myself away. The twins wore crisp, freshly ironed khaki, their long shorts slapping around their knees.

A breeze came in through the open windows and swirled around them as if they were already in the air, whizzing past our family and onto their next destination. They placed their hats on top of their heads, and Papa clapped each of them on the back.

"Be safe," he said.

The twins approached Ammi, and she placed a hand on each of their heads. "Make sure to write to us every day."

"We promise, Ma," they said at the same time, even though she wasn't their Ammi the way she was mine. The twins turned and saluted Papa, who saluted them in turn. Then they were gone in a flurry of whoops and laughs.

After they left, the kitchen was shrouded in a deafening silence. Papa kept staring at a point on the table and was only shaken from his reverie by Ammi's gentle hand on his shoulder.

"They'll be fine," she said. "They're good boys, made from good stock." She squeezed his shoulder.

"Will you be all right alone in this house with only Chotu?" Papa asked.

"Chotu and I will keep the house running," Ammi said. "We will manage."

Papa kissed Ammi's hand. I watched this loving exchange between them, the soft smiles on their faces, talking as if I wasn't in the room.

Then Papa smoothed the sleeves of his uniform. "It might be wise to send for your mother in Calcutta. She's alone, after all."

"No," Ammi said with the kind of finality that always shut Papa's mouth. She finally noticed me gripping the table.

"What is in Calcutta?" I asked.

Ammi shook her head. "Bad things. The whole city is haunted by a fearsome churail." Papa tut-tutted under his breath, but Ammi went on, "We can never go to Calcutta because if you do, the churail will get you." She twisted her fingers into claws and growled. It made me laugh. She beckoned me so I could put my arms around Papa's neck. I buried my face under his chin, sniffing the starch from his khaki uniform.

"I won't be far," Papa said. "Just an hour's train ride from here." He glanced up at Ammi. "However long this war lasts, I'll always be an hour from U.P." Outside, a jeep rumbled up to the house and emitted a nasal honk. Papa glanced at his watch. "I should go."

Ammi beheld Papa as he stood before her. She touched the cloth of his uniform and rubbed his mustache down. Beside her, I looked up in awe at Papa. My brave, courageous Papa, off to win the war for the whole world. Papa kissed Ammi on the forehead. "Just an hour away," he said again.

Ammi hugged him and shut her eyes, laying her head against Papa's heart. Then she stepped away from him and turned to me. "Go on," she said.

I stood to attention and saluted Papa, who saluted back with a bemused smile.

He squeezed me into a hug. "Pretty soon, you'll be too old for hugs, won't you?"

I hoped that would never happen.

Papa stepped away from us and took a last look around the house. Then, he too was gone in a cloud of dust. I stared at the front door, not sure if Papa would return.

Ammi frowned down at me. "Please don't do that," she said.

"Do what?"

"Please don't look as if it's the last time you'll see him. We'll see him again." She began to clear the table. "We'll see him again."

Almost weekly, the wails of the mothers and sisters and wives floated in through the open windows and circulated through the house, aided by the lazy movement of the ceiling fans. At first, Ammi waited until the egg boy brought her the news. Before handing him the money, she would start with the same line of questioning—"How?" she'd ask, followed by, "Where?"

The boy would give satisfactory answers: so-and-so's husband was killed by Pashtun gunmen in the Northwest Frontier, or someone's pilot brother accidentally flew his Wapiti into the mountains. Or another's daughter who bled to death from just one bullet to her leg. Ammi's mind would race, reconciling news of brigades, battalions, and regiments with details of where Papa and the twins were situated in the world. She'd clutch her throat and nod and pay the boy, who'd run off and deliver the news to another worried family.

After that, the news was simply handed around the neighborhood, something to share with everyone, no need for privacy or discretion. Then, when the next house was hit with bad news, families streamed out of their homes, servants in tow, to cry out in public to their god or gods.

Blasphemy, I thought. Was God really present during this jang-e-azam? And anyways, didn't He have a rather busy job pulling out the souls of the fallen soldiers when there were countless fallen at that?

Ammi and I stood in the doorway and watched a house across the road spew out its people onto the dusty, heat-laden street. A mother led the way, beating her breast, while her daughter gestured to the skies above. Ammi didn't hesitate. She ran out onto the street, dupatta fluttering behind her, straight into the grieving parade. I took off after her, wheezing under the dry sun.

"How?" Ammi asked, but the woman continued crying. Ammi clutched her shoulders. "How did it happen?"

The daughter pulled at Ammi's arms, her eyes wide with shock. "Burma." She shook her head in disbelief. "In the jungle. The jungle."

Ammi let the women go and stood aside as they trudged past. She giggled under her breath. "Burma," she said and wiped the sweat off her forehead with her dupatta. "Your papa is nowhere near there." She sighed, looking up at the sun. "The war will be over soon," she said. "And then we'll all be whole again."

But I didn't believe her. For years, it felt like all we ever talked about was the war. It used to feel so far away, but it kept creeping in closer and closer. Once it had touched all of our neighbors, how long before we were next?

Papa was out there all on his own. If I felt the war inching its way closer to us, Papa was fully immersed in it and would be for an untold amount of time.

I couldn't hide in our house and peek out the windows while Papa was out there in the open. I needed to do something about it.

In the afternoon, Ammi retired to the living room to plunk some optimistic notes on the piano. As the music drifted up through the floor, I packed a small gunny bag with clothes, then slipped down the backstairs to the kitchen to wrap up a few aloo parathas.

Ammi had stopped playing by now. She retired to her room to lie down for a dreamless nap, so I grabbed the moment and sneaked outside and shook the dust off my bicycle. The sun beat down on top of my head, its large disapproving eye watching me as I jumped aboard, setting the handlebars in the direction of DAV College.

As I approached the campus, a different sort of parade blocked the road. Solemn-looking students my brothers' age, male and female, shuffled past with flags and signs. I dismounted and watched them file past, tried to make sense of the large painted letters on their homemade signs—pieces of cloth held up on either side by sticks. The paint was still shiny and dripped down to leave drops in the dirt, but I could make out the English letters. "GO HOME," it read. I felt a prickle of fear on the back of my neck; I convinced myself those words weren't meant for me. Beyond the fringes of the crowd, policemen stood around, watching with a steely gaze, their jaws ticking. I ducked out of their sight. The rowdier ones jostled each other with their elbows. I searched the crowd for a familiar face.

Finally, I found our neighbor's son within the ranks and pulled my bicycle toward him, pushing through the crowd to tug on his sleeve. "Where can I find my brother?" I asked him.

"What are you doing here?" He looked around, glancing at the waiting policemen just out of reach. "You could get hurt."

"I need to find Muhammad," I said. "He's not here, is he?"

The neighbor's son sighed and pulled himself out of the crowd. I pushed my bicycle along and jogged after him until we'd arrived at the campus. Frantic, energized students swarmed the grounds, some running back the way I'd just come to join the protest. Our neighbor's son led me to a building with an arched hallway.

"Wait here. I'll get him."

It wasn't long until Muhammad appeared in the hallway. He turned several shades lighter and threw a hand to his chest when he saw me. "What's happened?" Muhammad asked. "Who's hurt?"

"No one," I said, but it wasn't entirely true. I'd seen yet another family lose their patriarch earlier that day. "Papa and Yusuf and Moosa are all right."

Of all my half-brothers, Muhammad looked like Papa the most. He had a high brow, dark, inquisitive eyes, and a soft mouth that belied his sensitive nature. Muhammad knelt and hugged me. "Don't ever scare me like that again," he said.

He led me to his dormitory. "Is Ma all right then?"

"We just miss Papa."

Muhammad smiled at me. "I miss him too."

He led me to his room, where the open windows let in a warm breeze. Muhammad sat on his bed and gestured to me to sit at the desk he shared with his roommate. "Why'd you come all the way here on your own then?"

"Only you will tell me about the war. Ammi never wants to talk about it," I said. "I won't," Muhammad said. Angry furrows appeared on his usually placid forehead. "That's all I do day and night. Jang, jang, jang. That's all my professors want to talk about, all my friends want to talk about. They come here trying to enlist us, steal us students, the future of this country, for God's sake. All for this stupid war. A war we didn't ask for, that we have no business fighting in. All for our captors." Muhammad sat with his fists in his lap. "We'll never be free."

"We aren't free?"

Muhammad stared at me. "It's a bit complicated to explain that to you right now."

"I'm twelve. I'm not a baby. You hate the war, and yet Papa and the twins are off fighting for our country."

"We aren't fighting for our country," Muhammad said. "Our country has, eh, 'owners'. And they are the ones in trouble. And because they own us, we have to help them."

"So that's a good thing," I said. "Papa and the twins are helping."

"I suppose." Muhammad sat back against the wall. "But our owners are up against some evil men. So yes, they are helping. And once we've helped our owners, hopefully, we'll be rewarded with freedom."

"I like that," I said, but Muhammad still looked troubled. "Ammi said the war would be over soon."

Muhammad took off his glasses and rubbed his eyes. "I hope so, Chotu. Your ammi will be worried. Let's get you home."

I didn't move. "I want to see Papa."

Muhammad stared out of the window for a moment. "You can't see him whenever you feel like it. I don't know where he is."

"You know where he is," I protested. "You do know."

Muhammad stood up at the sound of frenzied shouts from the other students. He settled into his usual world-weary slouch and opened the door, waving me out.

I glared up at him. "You don't understand. I have to see Papa so I can save him."

"Is that right?" Muhammad asked, a playful smirk on his face. "How are you going to save Papa?"

"You don't worry about the details." I puffed out my chest, feeling very brave at that moment. "Papa said he's only an hour away from here. I need you to take me to the train and help me get on board. I will handle the rest."

Muhammad shook his head. "Look—"

"I have to see Papa. I have to see him. If I don't see him, then something bad will happen to him." There was an embarrassing sting in my eyes, and then big ugly tears fell onto my cheeks. I wiped them away. "Why won't you help me?"

I stood in the doorway and held my arms out to either side, blocking Muhammad's path. "Just an hour's train ride, Papa promised."

"He isn't there," Muhammad spoke so quietly that I almost didn't hear him. A warm breeze fluttered into the room, but a chill surrounded me, turning me cold all over.

"He's gone. The regiment moved east."

"Where east?" I asked, constructing a hasty map of the world in my mind.

"Burma." Muhammad's voice was hoarse, and he rubbed his jaw. "I wasn't supposed to tell anyone, but you forced my hand."

Burma. I slumped against the door frame. "Papa lied to us." The tears were gone now, replaced by something else. The cold was inside me now.

"It isn't a lie if you're only shading the truth," Muhammad said. "Another complicated thing I'll have to explain when you're older."

I took hold of my bicycle. "Then we're going east."

"You're asking for a lot." Muhammad tried to stop me, but I flinched.

"Papa isn't asking for a lot," I said. "You sit here angry at the world and buried in your books while Papa and Yusuf and Moosa are out there fighting for their lives. And Ammi and I are alone in the house all by ourselves. Is there anything to you worth fighting for?"

Muhammad watched me as I quaked in front of him. "Since when did you become a little man?" He looked at his watch and sighed. "Okay, forget history class," he said. "I always hated history anyways."

I stood aside as Muhammad dug into his wardrobe and packed a small trunk. "Let's go before I change my mind."

He hurried out of the door, with me and my bike close behind.

At the train station, Muhammad asked for the schedules and balked when told how long it would take. "Four days?"

The station agent rolled his eyes. Muhammad glanced at his watch and muttered under his breath. "Forget about classes this week then." He turned back to the yawning agent. "Two tickets."

We headed for the platform, pushing past the others who were off on their own mysterious journeys. I wove and ducked to keep up with Muhammad. I'd never been on a train before and, as the crowds parted, the sight of one made me stop. The train was a menacing-looking python, its insides making loud clanging noises. It sat still on the tracks, held against its will. When it sighed, its maw released smoky clouds of soot.

Muhammad turned back and took hold of my arm. "It's easy to get lost here. Keep up."

He led me to our carriage. Once we were inside, Muhammad stashed my bicycle above us and let me sit next to the window. We settled against the seats and watched the compartment fill up with lone travelers, young couples in pairs, and families with mothers and fathers, their children racing each other and throwing themselves into their seats. The air had a particular scent of adventure.

"Where do you think they're going?" I asked.

"Wherever this train wants to take them." Muhammad pointed out of the window. "Watch how the country changes."

"You've taken this trip before?"

Muhammad smiled at a faraway memory. "We lived in Calcutta, where Papa used to teach. That's how he and your ammi met."

"I didn't know that. No one tells me anything."

"Hey." Muhammad nudged me with an elbow in my side. "You get slighted by the world too easily. You must work on that."

The train lurched forward and peeled away from the platform. I watched the world pass by like scenes on a reel. As I sat in my seat, I felt it keenly that since the moment I'd left home, I'd grown taller, my body had filled into my clothes better, my legs were long enough for my feet to touch the ground. I was a man now: chasing the world to find Papa and save him from the war.

The plains stretched out before me, melting together into browns and greens and beiges and blues. I felt dizzy and turned away from the window. "What about your ammi?" I asked. "How did she meet Papa?"

Muhammad munched on the aloo parathas I had brought along. "They didn't meet until the night of their wedding when they were presented side by side to the guests. My ammi snuck a glance at Papa when they laid a mirror at their feet." Muhammad smiled. "She thanked God he was handsome. Those were the times."

"Do you miss her?" I asked.

Muhammad settled back in the seat and shut his eyes. "I might sleep a while," he said. He tipped his head back and crossed his arms. I noticed a faint tremor in his lower lip.

The compartment had quieted by then. A drowsy wind blew through the windows and the passengers on the upper berths nodded off. The train sped onward; its chugging and clanking eventually lulled me to sleep.

A few days later, we arrived in Calcutta thirsty and sore and stumbled off the train into a heavy, wet heat. Sweat clung to our backs and chests in minutes, creating unsightly pools in our armpits. I gripped my bicycle with sweaty palms as passengers left the station and poured out onto the streets, heading in all directions.

We staggered onto the main road, stifled on either side by tall buildings and storefronts. I noticed that the streetlights were covered on top with dark paper and tugged on Muhammad's sleeve to show him, but Muhammad was busy heading for a tonga. It was sitting idle like it had been waiting for us all along.

We slid in behind the driver.

"We need to go to the medical college," Muhammad said in his best Bengali. "Dr. Madhu Bannerji, please."

"Hain?" The driver turned around to stare at us. "Am I supposed to know who that is?"

Muhammad flushed, and a sheepish grin appeared on his face. "No, bhaisaab, no. Just take us to the college."

The driver grunted and whipped the horse's behind. The tonga shuddered to life.

"Am I supposed to know who that is?" I asked.

"He's very well connected in the Congress Party. And he knows our abbu. There are army bases here in the city. Abbu had to come through here if he's in Burma."

I sat back satisfied, feeling ever closer to Papa. As the tonga clip-clopped along, I watched the city unveil itself. Buildings towered over narrow twisting streets. Children chased each other around their parents' legs by the side of the road. Across one street, a man sat cross-legged on the ground, smoking a bidi and glaring at those who walked past. Smartly dressed women clad in fine saris strutted past, and I immediately thought of Ammi. What had she said about a fearsome churail ruling over the city? I kept a lookout as traffic eased up on either side of us. Empty tongas whizzed past, and the shops shuttered their windows. The city seemed to be slowly taking itself to bed.

Then, a razor-sharp siren tore through the night air. The tonga jerked, rattling us in the back, then swerved to avoid a herd of running people. Shouts and screams were coming from all directions; I didn't know which way to look. Another wail rang out. The horse reared up, and the tonga screeched to a halt. I gripped the seat underneath me.

"What's happening, bhaisaab?" Muhammad asked.

The driver stared up at the sky, his eyes white with fear. We looked up, too. A third wail rang out amid the chaos. The driver cursed under his breath and hopped out of his seat, pulling on the horse's reins. He waved at us. "Get out!" he screamed, then looked up at the sky again. "Get out!"

Muhammad pulled me out after him, and we tumbled out onto the road together. All around us, people frantically dashed in different directions. Muhammad dug into his pockets for money, but the driver waved him away.

"For God's sake, take shelter," he shouted and pulled his horse away.

"I don't know where to go," Muhammad panicked as another siren wailed. He took my hand, and we joined a group of people stampeding to the end of the road.

We were jostled to-and-fro, and suddenly, Muhammad's hand snapped out of my grip. I groped the air for Muhammad, but ended up slapping my hand against unfamiliar arms and legs. In the frenzy, I saw terrified, tear-stained faces; I still see them sometimes in my dreams. But there was no Muhammad. I ran onward in the dark, searching for my brother.

"Bhaiya!"

An arm circled my shoulder, and I looked up into the face of a kindly woman. She held onto her daughter with her other arm.

"Come with me." She pulled the two of us through the entrance of a building at the end of the road.

I resisted. "My brother," I said, reaching behind me as if he were still there.

"There'll be nothing left of either of you if you don't hurry," she said and dragged me into a nearby store, where several others were heading for the basement. We plunged into the darkness even as we heard muffled sirens from the outside. The air reeked of nervous sweat. I struggled to breathe as the woman led me to a corner and pulled me down next to her. She held her daughter and me close to her chest and, for a moment, my heart stopped hammering. I thought of Ammi, nestled against this woman.

Suddenly, I grew alert and wary of my surroundings, wondering if Muhammad was somewhere in the shelter when the first bomb shattered the storefront above us.

The blast echoed in our room, followed by the crackle of debris falling and the groan of concrete splitting.

A small hand reached for mine, and I squeezed it back. In the dark, the only sounds were of delirious panting and crying, followed by a sickening silence.

I awoke alone. Bright sunlight from the door would momentarily light up the shelter as it swung open and shut, immersing the room in total darkness and then intense illumination. I watched others trudge up the stairs and disappear into the light.

"Bhaiya?" I called, my raspy voice strange to me, but Muhammad didn't appear.

I stood up only to find that my wobbly legs barely supported me. With one unsteady step after another, I followed the others up the stairs and emerged into the grocery store where shelves had been knocked backward as if shoved by an unseen hand. A crude path was made on the ground: shattered glass and spoiled food swept aside to allow people to walk.

I staggered out into the bright morning sun. Slow-walking city folk shambled from store to store to survey the damage. Their eyes were wide and despondent, looking at one another for answers. The front of the grocery store was riddled with holes, and a large crater had opened up in the ground. A group of strangers stared into it as if it might provide them with some answers. The woman and her daughter were nowhere in sight.

I walked in a daze across the street and stared up at the sky. It was bright and hot; a few wisps of cloud marred the blazing blue. There was no sign of the threat from the night before.

The phantoms who'd flown above the city to destroy it were gone. At the end of the street, a crowd had gathered in a circle. Feeling a jolt in my stomach, I pushed forward to the center. Two dead cows lay on the ground, their feet sticking straight up, their eyes wide open, and tongues lolling out of their mouths. I doubled over, hot bile rising in my chest. I stepped away from the crowd and headed back to where I thought the tonga had dropped us off the night before.

The tonga was gone, and so were my clothes and other belongings. I felt my tongue baked dry against the roof of my mouth, like the dead cows I'd seen moments ago. I sat down on the footpath and hugged my trembling knees.

"Bhaiya," I called out, shielding my eyes from the sun and expecting Muhammad to come running from the crowd. But no one paid me any mind.

I glanced down at the rubble beside me and found a familiar tire sticking out of the dirt. Large, crude stones weighed it down. I pushed them off, then dusted away sand and concrete powder to reveal my beloved bicycle. I lifted it out and shook it clean, then pinched the tires and gave the gears a once-over. There wasn't a scratch on it, and I almost wept with joy. Didn't Ammi always say miracles happened when they were least expected?

I wheeled my bicycle to the nearest police officer, who was busy scribbling notes and intermittently staring up at the sky. "How can I get to the medical college?" I asked. The police officer knelt, his mustache quivering.

"Are you hurt?" He scanned my face and took hold of my arm to investigate.

"No. I have to meet my uncle at the college."

The police officer nodded. He jotted a note, then ripped the sheet off his notepad and handed it to me. "It isn't too far," he said, pointing to the end of the street. I hopped on my bicycle and scanned the directions, then crumpled the paper up and shoved it into my front pocket. "Be safe," the policeman called after me.

My arms shook as I pumped my legs to get to the college as fast as possible. Muhammad was there; I was sure of it. He must have been just a few feet ahead of me all this time. Around me, students sauntered past, back to their mundane routines as if nothing had happened to the city the night before.

When I arrived at the college, I was greeted by zig-zag trenches gouged into the earth. I got off my bicycle and followed the tracks to the front of the campus. There, three youths were digging up the ground, cussing and teasing each other.

"Where is Dr. Bannerji?" I asked, clearing my throat so as not to squeak.

A student around Muhammad's age glared up at me, sweat dribbling into his eyes. "You're a little young for college." The other boys laughed.

"He's my uncle," I said. "Our family was hurt in the bombing last night."

The boy turned pale while the other two quieted down. He tossed his shovel and struggled out of the trench, his friends hoisting him up from beneath. I stepped aside as the boy brushed the dirt from his shirt and pants.

"Follow me."

He led the way into a building and then, with a finger blackened with earth, pointed down an empty hallway to a classroom at the end. "You'll find him in there."

I left my bicycle against the wall and waded through a trickle of students until I'd reached the classroom. I peeked in, but there was no Muhammad in sight, only a solitary man in an empty room leaning into the radio on his desk. He was younger than I had imagined—rather than Papa's age, he looked closer to Ammi's. He was a rich shade of brown, with broad shoulders and a thick head of hair, parted to one side and gelled back.

He was so absorbed by the disembodied voice streaming out of his radio that he didn't notice me. I stepped inside to have a look around. Desks crowded against each other, jockeying for space in the room. There was a model of the inside of a man's chest at the head of the room. Next to that hung a poster of the skeletal makeup of the human body. These models made me feel more queasy than I did emerging from the shelter.

The voice on the radio became clearer. The strange passion of the speaker made my skin itch. "This is Subhash Chandra Bose calling out to you over the Azad Hind Radio. Do not be confused by Japan's bombing of Calcutta. I appeal to you not to confuse the Japanese with our true enemies—the British and the British Empire. Their leaders think we Muslims, Hindus, and Sikhs cannot peacefully coexist. How can we, after centuries of outsiders meddling in our affairs? By dividing us, they will conquer us. And that is why we must come together, create our own army, a national Indian Army. Our independence will be supported and strengthened by the Axis Powers of Germany, Italy, and Japan if we only lend our support . . ."

Dr. Bannerji jumped when he realized I was there, and turned off the radio.

"Who are you?" he asked, mopping his brow with a crumpled kerchief. I told him that my brother and I came to see him from Cawnpore and that he knew my papa.

Dr. Bannerji sat back against his chair. "So you are Haroon. Muhammad was here last night after the raid. He had no idea where you went after you were separated. But I'm afraid he's gone."

Tears gathered in my eyes. "Where is he?"

"After the bombing, we searched the town for you with no luck. I took him back to the station this morning."

Dr. Bannerji came around the desk. "I told him I'd find you, but it looks like you found me." I shook with sadness and Dr. Bannerji patted my shoulder.

"Is he safe then?"

"Anywhere is safer than here. Except for the Front," he said with a dark laugh. He took a seat at one of the desks and gestured for me to do the same. "You want to find your father, is that right?"

"I want to see him," I said. "I have to see him."

Bannerji pinched the tip of his mustache and shook his head. "It's not easy to storm into the war seeking one lone man among hundreds, nay thousands."

I scowled at the man, and he shifted in his seat.

"I know you came here with a purpose. But you'll have to be patient until I can find help. I have contacts. Over in Burma." Dr. Bannerji glanced at the radio.

"I won't leave without Papa. I'll stay here and wait as long as I have to." I squeezed my hands into fists and beat my thighs. "They'll come and try to take me away. No one understands what I've gone through to see Papa."

Dr. Bannerji sighed. "He can't return home just because you want him to. I know your father. He would never give up being a soldier. He'd give up anything but that. Except maybe your mother," he said with a grin.

"You know my ammi?"

Dr. Bannerji scanned my face. "You look more like her than your father." His smile faltered. "I must send word to your brother that I found you." He stood up. "Until then, I know somewhere you can stay."

I wouldn't move.

"Until I can locate your father."

"Promise?" I asked. "Promise me that you'll find him."

"Achha, baba. Whew, Muhammad told me you were stubborn. Just like your mother." I didn't know what that meant.

I followed Dr. Bannerji out of the classroom and back onto the campus. We climbed into a tonga, and as I sat back gripping my knees, I remembered my last tonga ride in the city. But this one was without bombs or sirens or fear. As we drove back through the city center, we saw massive lines forming outside the train station. People carried large bundles of cloth on their heads as they queued up, while some pulled carts filled with furniture and bedding. Dr. Bannerji tsk-tsked at the sight.

The tonga made its way through the columns of defeated people and turned into a quiet street lined with rows of large houses. "Ah!" Dr. Bannerji exclaimed and patted the driver on the back. The tonga stopped outside a three-story building, each layer painted a different color and dotted with several pairs of dark windows for eyes. While Dr. Bannerji settled the fare, I pulled my bicycle out of the tonga and led it up to the house.

"You can stay here until I get ahold of your papa," Bannerji said. We walked up to the door together, and before we could knock, it swung open on its own. A cold breeze crept out of the house and ticked my ankles. The inside of the house was covered in shadows.

A hoarse voice called out, "Who's there?"

"Madhu Bannerji here, with your grandson."

"What?"

The question crawled back into my throat as a woman appeared in the doorway.

She had a regal bearing—a thick braid wound its way from the top of her head to her lower back, with bands of gray riding the waves and losing themselves in her plait. She folded her hands in front of her and glared at us, her bloodshot eyes lined with kohl.

"Oh," she said when her eyes settled on me. "She's sent her son."

Dr. Bannerji tensed next to me. "Yes, yes she did." He clapped me on the back.

"Hmm," the woman said. "They must be having trouble at home."

"We aren't," I retorted.

"She'll be sending for him soon." Dr. Bannerji's eyes indicated I shouldn't question him.

"All right." The woman crooked an already bent finger in my direction. "Come inside like a good boy and meet your grandmother."

Dr. Bannerji pushed me forward and backed away to the tonga. My newfound grandmother stepped aside and waited for me to enter the house before slamming the door with a sharp crack.

Once inside, I realized why the place was shrouded in shadows. Every window in the house was covered with dark crepe paper. My grandmother observed my curiosity and crossed her arms.

"My cowardly servants fled the city. Your poor dear grandmother has no one. Will you be a good grandson and take care of her?"

"Yes, Naani."

I still marvel at the manners my ammi had taught me. I don't know if I'd behave the same way if it happened to me now.

"Good. Go outside and get me some water."

"From where?" I asked.

"From the well. It'll be nice and cold for your dear grandmother." She held up three bony fingers and ticked them off. "Then I want you to do the washing, sweep the floors, and come upstairs to fan me while I sleep."

"Yes, Naani."

My grandmother's smile stretched across her face, her teeth stained orange from chewing paan. I recalled Ammi's words with a shudder—I was looking right at the Churail of Calcutta.

"Go."

I ran out to fetch my grandmother some water.

# SIX

# THE DIARY

The kitchen smelled glorious when Maera and Jimmy walked in. Her stomach rumbled in response. The mothers had their backs turned; they were muttering to each other and busying themselves at the stove.

Aisha Khala turned and pointed at Jimmy. "The chutney is in a jar in the fridge—make the raita. And you," she faced Maera as she wiped her eyes, "can you slice these onions for the kachumber? Your glasses must act as a shield."

Maera and Jimmy went their separate ways. While Jimmy combined yogurt and chutney to whip up the raita, Maera set to work preparing the kachumber, mixing chopped tomatoes and cucumbers and onions. She sneaked a glance at her mother, who serenely spooned biryani into a small casserole dish.

"Is it okay if we sit outside tonight?" Maera asked.

The mothers stopped what they were doing to stare at her, their mom-sense somehow seeing right through her.

"Only because it's so nice out. We should take advantage of it before it gets too hot." Maera glared at Jimmy.

"I'd love to," he said, his voice cracking. He cleared his throat. "It's a beautiful night."

Ammi turned back to the large wooden spoon in her hand. "I'd like that," she said.

Maera took plates down from the cupboard and eyed Jimmy, motioning for him to follow her with the raita. Once they were outside, she whispered, "Go get the diary. Hide it in your shirt or something."

Jimmy stared at the greenhouse. "I don't know if I'm ready."

"It's now or never."

She turned him around to face the house. Jimmy hurried inside while Maera took her time arranging the plates and cutlery on the table, even though she knew she'd be digging in with her hands, utensils optional.

The mothers emerged outside, Ammi carrying the biryani and Aisha Khala the kachumber and a pitcher of lemonade. Trailing after them was Jimmy, now sporting a light jacket, his left arm crooked at his side.

"Why are you wearing that?" Aisha Khala asked with a laugh.

"It's a little cold," Jimmy said.

Maera chuckled a little too loud. "Maybe he's not used to temperate weather."

"Hmm," Ammi said.

Maera heaped her plate with biryani, laid the kachumber on the side, and doused it all in raita. She dug in with her fingers and got to work. A few mouthfuls later, she noticed the greenhouse's imposing presence in her backyard. She'd forgotten it was there; it had gotten comfortable and decided to become a regular feature of her backyard.

"It's not too warm out. I like it," Ammi said in between bites. "I don't know why we don't sit out here more often."

"I think that's the most you've spoken to all of us. Is your cold heart melting?" Aisha Khala pursed her lips at Ammi, then giggled. "You sound like the old Amna again."

Ammi stared at her sister for a moment. "Maybe I am the old Amna," she said and gave her twin a rare smile.

Once the biryani was consumed and the dishes put away, the mothers retired to the living room to watch a drama on TV. Maera and Jimmy sat cross-legged in the grass facing the greenhouse.

Jimmy thumbed through the diary while Maera peeked at the cracked and worn pages, making out some of the ornate curls as letters of the Urdu alphabet and cursing herself for being unable to understand them. Jimmy read in silence beside her, caressing each page as he turned it.

"What does it say?" Maera asked in a whisper as if the greenhouse could hear her and realize they were conspiring against it.

"It's a story," Jimmy replied. "A journey. But it's not in any order."

"That doesn't tell me anything." Maera sat back, feeling slightly dejected.

Jimmy stared at the book, unblinking. "It's the way our naana chose to write it. If he wanted to tell us about the greenhouse, then it should be in here." He muttered something else and began reading out loud.

Maera lay down in the grass next to him, the blades pricking her back. She stared up at the hazy wisps of clouds blotting out the stars.

Jimmy spoke again to translate some of what he'd read. "Our naana went on a journey when he was twelve years old. He was searching for his father."

Maera shut her eyes and tried to imagine a younger version of her grandfather. "The one who fought in the war."

"Yes," Jimmy said. "Instead, he found his grandmother. He writes she was the Churail of Calcutta."

"Seriously?" Maera propped herself up on her elbows and stifled a laugh. "A touch dramatic, no?"

"That's what he wrote." Jimmy shrugged and set the diary down.

"Churailain don't exist."

Jimmy seemed to chew on his words. "I've heard stories."

"Uh-huh. Stories to scare us kids into submission." She poked his side. "What happened next?"

Jimmy looked down at his lap. "That's only the beginning. I haven't read very far."

Maera stood up and brushed the grass from her shalwar. Her gaze lingered on the greenhouse. "That didn't tell us anything," she said. "What does it say about this thing and how to get inside of it?"

He folded a corner. "We have to be patient if we want to know everything. I skipped to the last page; he stopped writing in this diary around 1947, well before our moms were born. It won't mention us or Asad or anything recent."

"Ugh, it won't mention the night he went missing. That's the most important thing."

"We were given this diary for a reason. Even if it doesn't mention Asad, I want to know what happened to Naana, too." Jimmy stared up at Maera, his eyes glassy and bloodshot. "Ever since I saw the greenhouse again, one memory keeps pulling at me. That last night we saw Asad. I remember waking up and feeling so scared."

The memory hit Maera like a landslide. She swayed on the spot.

"I do too. We'd all been sleeping on the roof because it was too hot to stay in the rooms, remember? I woke up, and Asad was gone."

He nodded. "Then there was just panic and tears. We never saw him again."

"I'm not allowed to talk about him, but that's all I want to do lately." Maera sounded distant.

Jimmy's eyebrows knotted together. "It's important not to forget someone."

Maera shrugged. "But reliving his disappearance? That's not fun."

"We have to relive it." Jimmy hauled himself up, tucking the diary under one arm. He approached the greenhouse door and held out a hand to touch it, his fingers hovering inches from the glass. "It wants us to."

Maera stood next to Jimmy and stared up at the monster. "I think if that diary doesn't tell us what happened to Asad, this greenhouse will."

# SEVEN

# THE ENTRY

The mothers lay half-asleep on the couch. They were draped on either side of the sofa, their bodies balled up under the throw. Only their feet were outside, toes snaking to touch the other's foot. Ammi's eyes were shut, while Aisha Khala's head nodded as she struggled to keep her eyes open. Maera and Jimmy stood over them like disapproving parents, hands on their hips, clicking their tongues and sighing loud enough for their mothers to hear.

"Jet lag," Aisha Khala explained and shook her head, attempting to rouse herself.

"I think you should go to bed," Jimmy said, eyeing his mother.

Maera's phone buzzed. She left Jimmy to handle the mothers and crept away to the front door to let Sara in.

"I made it," Sara said in between pants. She was carrying a stuffed backpack, and a sheen of sweat covered her face. "Tried to get here as fast as I could."

"Shh." Maera snuck a glance back at the living room.

"It's okay. I told my mom you needed me. She understood."

"What do you mean by that?"

Sara hitched the backpack further up her shoulder. "You know, you guys are in mourning. She said to stay for as long as you needed me."

Maera crossed her arms. "Bigger things are going on than us 'mourning'."

"Your naana just died," Sara said, but Maera shushed her. "Go put your stuff in my room, and then we're going outside and getting into that thing,"

Sara instead glanced behind Maera.

"What is it?" Maera turned around to find both Ammi and Aisha Khala standing behind her. She stepped back and waited to see if Ammi had heard them, but she only blinked her weary eyes at them.

"Is it okay if I stay for a few days?" Sara asked.

"Your ammi doesn't mind?"

"No, she thought it was a good idea. Because—"

She glanced at Maera.

Ammi moved forward and hugged Sara. "Thank you, mera beta."

"Bedtime!" Aisha Khala shouted and stumbled down the hall. Ammi followed her. Maera waited until the bedroom door was shut.

"You," she turned to Sara. "drop your stuff in my room." Sara nodded and brushed past her up the stairs. "And you," Maera said to Jimmy, "get the diary and meet me outside."

They scattered to follow her orders, and Maera didn't waste another moment. She changed out of her shalwar kameez into an old pair of jeans and a ratty T-shirt, then headed straight down into the kitchen and out the patio door.

The greenhouse sat still and imposing in the dark, cutting a jagged shape against the night sky and glowing with a swirling, muddled light. Maera walked around the structure and knocked on the glass. The fronds stirred for a moment, then fell still. She peered in, but there was nothing besides the usual leaves, trees, and vines.

She returned to the front of the greenhouse and heard the patio door slide shut. Jimmy and Sara joined Maera, and the three of them stared up at the monster together.

Just then, the fence creaked, and Sara flinched.

"What was that?" she whispered.

Maera blushed, thankful it was too dark for anyone to notice. "It's Rob from next door."

"What?" Jimmy and Sara asked together.

Rob strode up to them with a black backpack slung over a shoulder. Maera's breath caught in her chest; she was shocked at how much she enjoyed feasting her eyes on this upgrade of young Bobby.

"Sara?" Rob squinted. "I haven't seen you in years."

Sara stared hard at Maera, waiting for her response. Maera fidgeted with her wristwatch. "I asked him to help." She avoided the dark look Sara gave her.

Maera took hold of Jimmy's arm and pushed him forward. "This is my cousin Jamal."

"It's Jimmy." Sara and Jimmy corrected her at the same time, and Sara smiled at the ground.

Rob shook Jimmy's limp hand, then turned to Maera. "You have a team now. You got a plan?"

Maera chewed on her bottom lip. "Let's start with the door?"

She strode up to the entrance and curled her fingers around the handle. It was hot, as if a phantom hand had already warmed it with its touch.

"Here we go."

Maera pulled the handle down. The door was locked. She tried pulling the handle up, then jiggling it, but it was stuck. She kicked the door. "What do you want?"

Sara touched her shoulder, but Maera shrugged her hand away. Then, before anyone could stop her, Maera sped around to the side of the greenhouse and slapped the glass hard. "Why are you doing this?"

Rob was beside her, pulling her away. "Let me help. I brought tools."

He knelt to unzip his backpack and pulled out a ball of twine, a box cutter, a hammer, and several pairs of gloves. The rest of his stuff rattled around inside.

"Wow, okay."

Rob handed Maera the hammer. "Maybe we can start by shattering the door since it's a separate piece. It won't break the rest of the greenhouse, just the glass door."

Sara and Jimmy stood in front of the door. Sara hugged herself. "What's the point of this thing here if we can't get in?"

Maera gripped the hammer and pushed between them without a word.

"Don't do it!" Jimmy exclaimed when he spotted the tool.

It was too late. Maera swung at the door.

The hammer landed on the glass with a neat crack, but the glass remained undisturbed. Maera lunged at it again. Still, the glass didn't break. She tried a third time. This time, the glass warped under the hammer, then flung Maera back. She fell in a heap; the stars whirled above her in the night sky.

Sara and Jimmy rushed to her side and hauled her up. Maera ran back to the greenhouse with her fists extended. She pummeled the door, feeling the vibrations push back against her. Finally, Maera ran out of steam and sank to her knees, pressing her forehead against the warm glass.

"Please let me in. I need to know. Please," she whispered. Her face was wet with tears. She didn't know when she'd started crying. "I need to know what happened to him."

The lock clicked. Maera crawled away from the greenhouse as the handle jerked downward. Then the hinges loosened, and the door swung outward.

"Did not expect that to happen," Rob said, taking a big step back.

Maera stood up and wiped her tears. "I don't know how long it'll stay open for us. Let's go."

The four of them stepped into the greenhouse together.

# THE TRAIN TO BURMA

Bengal, India, 1943

I tottered on my bicycle on my way to the river with Naani's laundry wrapped in a tight ball and perched atop my head, which I held in place with one hand. My other hand steered the bicycle through the street, weaving through pedestrians, avoiding the tongas and cars that crowded the narrow roads.

As I sped onward, away from the city center, I could smell the salty human scent of the Ganges. It tickled my nostrils. I slowed down and shifted the bundle onto my lap. The bicycle wobbled, and I took control with both hands, pointing it in the direction of the river's edge, where several women were already up to their knees soaking lumps of cloth.

In the beginning, they'd smile askance at the strange boy washing an old woman's undergarments, but as I returned week after week, they soon forgot I existed. I was one of them now. I left the bicycle resting against a low wall, then stepped into the knee-high water and doused Naani's clothes.

Pushing the laundry deep into the water, I felt a twinge in my spine that made me stand straight up. Like ghosts, Naani's clothes surfaced and floated around my thighs. I rubbed the small of my back, but the pain would disappear and return in a different spot, as some sort of cruel joke. I bent over again and cringed at the pain, then went through my list for the day to distract myself: after washing, I needed to sweep the floors, beat the dust out of the carpets, and cook Naani a simple meal of boiled vegetables and rice. It would be nearly midnight before I'd be able to drag my weary body into bed. And then I'd have to be up before the sun rose to fill Naani's washbasin for her morning prayers.

A tear led a trail to the tip of my nose and dropped into the river without a sound. I continued washing the clothes, wringing them out and beating them mercilessly against the stones until they were thoroughly cleaned.

Once I returned to Naani's house, I carried the damp bundle, now heavy with water, on top of my head and to the back garden. I shook the water out and hung Naani's clothes and sheets on a clothesline.

Naani called out to me from the darkened recesses of the house. "That didn't take long at all. Next time, wash them longer. I better not see another stain."

I grumbled under my breath. If she didn't spit so much when she talked—paan juice spewing out haphazardly onto everything—I wouldn't have to scrub her clothes even harder.

I hung up the last of her sheets and stepped into the house. The shadows within moved, and I was struck by a sudden urge to rip out all the blackout paper taped against the windows to bring natural light back into the house and give it some life.

"Come here," Naani called from her room. I peeked in to see her lying on her bed with her hands folded on her stomach. "Work the fan until I fall asleep," she commanded, nodding at the rope beside the bed.

I untied the rope so that it was taut against me, then pulled and pulled as the fan swayed above Naani. I studied her face, watching her usual grimace melt away into tired contentedness.

"Child," she spoke in a sweet, warm voice and opened her eyes. She looked at me with an unfocused gaze.

I stopped and stared and then offered her a small smile.

Naani blinked a few times, then closed her eyes. "I thought you were someone else." She waved her hand. "Continue."

When Naani finally fell asleep, mumbling complaints in her dreams, I tied the rope back onto its hook and slipped out of the room. I glanced around the house, at the unused furniture that was swiftly gathering dust, at the empty bedrooms, and focused on the quiet around me. Naani continued to snore, oblivious to where I was or what I intended to do next.

I crept out of the house and hopped aboard my trusty bicycle, hoping my grandmother didn't hear the clicking sounds coming from the wheels. I stopped and waited for her to come running, brandishing her skeletal fists at me. But deep inside the house, she continued to sleep. I pushed into the pedals and took off toward the train station, the one from which Muhammad and I had emerged so many months ago.

It was late afternoon, and the station was teeming with harried passengers traveling in and out of the station, bumping into me as I made my way to the ticket booth. I stood at the end of the line, preparing to beg for a ticket if I had to, but as the queue grew longer behind me, I spotted a family at the front walk away with their tickets. I hopped out of the line and followed them, keeping close enough that we'd all seem like we were traveling together. The family filed into a third-class compartment, but I chose a different one for myself. I wheeled my bicycle in and sat in the very back.

Somehow, in some way, I was going to get to Papa. I'd been praying every night that Dr. Bannerji would bring me some news. But after my first day in Calcutta, I never saw the man again. Perhaps it was the tiny pit of guilt in the center of my stomach that made me stay longer with Naani than I intended—she was the only grandparent I'd ever met. But I'd waited too long, and I had wasted too much time. Papa was in Burma, and now I was going to do what I'd set out to do long ago: I'd find Papa and save him from the war.

The train crawled out of the station, then picked up speed. Lush greenery swayed outside of the window, moving aside for the train to pass. An old man next to me dozed with his head tilted back and his mouth hanging open.

A ticket collector entered our compartment, dressed in a black hat and a white coat. His tired-looking eyes scanned the carriage before he went person to person, shouting, "Ticket, ticket!" I stiffened in my seat while the old man next to me continued to snore.

When the ticket collector approached, I scooted closer to the sleeping man and spoke up in broken Bengali, thankful for the bits I'd learned from Ammi. "He has the tickets. But see how he sleeps?" I grinned. "It's impossible to wake him."

The ticket collector eyed the two of us and asked, "Where are you going?"

"We're both going to Burma to see my papa."

The ticket collector scratched his chin. "I'll come to get you when we arrive at your station." The train jostled him as he moved on to the next compartment.

I slumped against my seat and shut my eyes, only to be shaken awake by the ticket collector. The old man beside me was gone. "Just as I thought," the ticket collector said. "You looked like a runaway."

I peered out of the window as the train chugged along. Night had blackened the earth. "Am I in Burma?"

"Wrong train. We're headed to the south of Bengal. I need to get you back on the right train home."

"I won't go back," I said. "I have to see my papa."

The train slowed down. The few left in the compartment pushed the ticket collector aside and hustled out of the train.

"You'll have to come with me first."

We stepped down from the train and walked into the station. I followed the ticket collector to the station office. As I waited for him outside, I opened my mouth and took in a deep breath. The jungle was close; I could taste the dense vegetation in the air.

The ticket collector returned and frowned at me. "Where did you come from?" I told him I came from Calcutta.

The ticket collector raised his brows. "You're all by yourself?"

"Can you take me to my papa now?" I asked again.

The ticket collector scratched his chin again, a shadow of stubble forming on his face. "I'll take you to your papa tomorrow. It's very late now."

I watched the train depart with a mournful squeal. "I have to see him now."

"I know you do." The ticket collector glanced at the departing train. "But first, you need a roof over your head. You can't be alone out here by yourself."

"The very first thing in the morning?" I asked.

The ticket collector sighed. "Achha, baba, first thing in the morning."

I followed the ticket collector out of the station. "Aren't you going to get a tonga?" I asked, looking around the quiet road. Fellow passengers from the train were walking ahead of us.

"I like to walk."

It was then that I noticed the frayed hem of the ticket collector's coat and the loose threads that dangled from his sleeves. Instead of close-toed shoes, the ticket collector wore chappals; his feet were dusty and cracked at the heel. I followed along, leading my faithful bicycle onto the main road from where tranquil fields and clusters of leafy trees stretched out as far as the eye could see.

When an hour had passed and the night had deepened around us, we finally entered a village. I was out of breath, and I wiped the sweat from my forehead and neck. "Where are we?" I asked, staring at cows and chickens straggling across the road, followed by a lone villager.

The ticket collector smiled and spread his arms out wide. "My village. Kallikakundu."

I followed him to an oblong mud hut with a curved thatched roof. Two windows on either side of the door were crisscrossed with wooden sticks, far from the metal grating I remembered barring my windows back home. A woman emerged to greet the ticket collector. She shot a worried look in my direction, followed by a questioning glance at her husband.

"I found him on the train. He's on the hunt for his father."

"That's why I was in Calcutta," I added as I leaned my bicycle against the side of the hut. "He's in Burma. He's a soldier."

"You're out here all by yourself?" the woman asked.

"I'm not afraid of anything."

The woman looked at her husband again. "You must be hungry," she said to me. "Why don't you eat and get some rest, and we'll take you to your papa in the morning. Come along."

Before I could enter the house, I was distracted by a scraping sound outside. Something rustled the leaves in the cluster of trees beside the house, breaking twigs as it moved. I squinted in the dark and thought I saw a shadow. I edged closer, but the ticket collector stepped back outside and placed a heavy hand on my shoulder. When I turned to look at the trees, there was nothing there.

The hut was minuscule, much smaller than what I was used to, but it smelled of cooking and warmth, just like any home. Their home was one large room with an alcove for a kitchen, and two small nooks as bedrooms, tucked into the side and separated by half a wall. The hut had sparse wooden furniture, painted in vivid colors, and though the carpet under my feet was threadbare, its colorful weave brightened it.

I thought back to my own large house. Before living as Naani's servant, I never had to ask for anything—my every need was provided for by my parents. On the other hand, the ticket collector's family lived a far humbler life in a tiny village, toiling hard for everything they owned. The thought of this disparity shamed me, and I felt like an unholy outsider, dirtying the ticket collector's home with my privileged presence.

In the light of the hurricane lamps that cast long, flickering shadows, I spotted a striking set of dark eyes staring at me. They belonged to a girl about my age.

"Baba, who is this?" she asked, pointing directly at me.

"A lost boy."

Before I could correct him, he clapped me on the back. "You must be hungry."

My stomach growled. I realized that I hadn't eaten since morning.

"Please sit." The ticket collector led me to the middle of the hut, where the mother and the girl set plates on the floor.

I was disappointed when the girl sat across from me rather than next to me. My face grew hot, and I was certain she could sense my inner turmoil. I stared at my dinner instead—two lumps of pumpkin and daal on a small clay plate.

"I'm sorry," the mother said. "We don't have rice."

"I—I don't mind."

"It's too expensive," the girl explained.

"Don't," the ticket collector warned her. "I told you not to speak of it again."

"They're trying to starve us," the girl said to me. My heart beat faster when the girl looked me in the eye.

"No one is trying to starve us," the ticket collector said in a stern tone.

"The British Army is," the girl went on. "Took away and destroyed our ships, and now no one can afford rice anymore." She glanced at the windows as if the army stood right outside listening to her. "Then our corrupt landowners make Ma work and work in the fields and let us starve."

I swallowed a nugget of pumpkin and stared back at her wide-eyed, my ignorance rendering me mute.

"We are not starving," her mother spoke up. "Don't tell tales." She gave a nervous laugh. "Especially not in front of our guest."

"I'm not telling tales," the girl said. "I heard the students talking about it in the village, and they know everything."

The ticket collector gave the girl a surly look. He wagged a finger at her. "I told you not to listen to gossip. You mind your business and let them talk all they want."

The girl chewed her food angrily, glaring at the floor. I dug in and was done with the modest meal in seconds.

"You must not have had your mother's food in a while," the mother said as I set my plate back on the ground. I told them I hadn't seen her in a long while.

"Where has she gone?" the girl asked but looked down when her parents frowned at her.

I sat forward, elbows on knees. "I left U.P. to find my papa. Instead, I found my naani. I thought I found a friend in Doctor Bannerji, that he would help me, but he left me with my grandmother instead." My lip curled; I couldn't help it.

"Is she not nice to you?" the girl piped up and then fell silent again with a look from her parents.

I shrugged and didn't respond.

Dinner complete, mother and daughter piled the plates and took them away to be scrubbed.

"I can help," I offered, but the mother shook her head.

"It's women's work," she said with a smile. The girl glowered at her mother, then at me.

"I've scrubbed dishes before," I called to their retreating backs, ready to tell them about the hours spent cooking and cleaning for Naani, but neither acknowledged me.

The ticket collector showed me to the smaller of the two bedrooms where a charpai was set out. "This is my daughter's room," he said. "You can sleep here, and we will take the other one."

"I can't have this to myself," I protested. "I'll sleep on the floor."

"You are our guest. Please take the room." He waited until I settled myself on the charpai before leaving with the hurricane lamp, the light bobbing after him.

The dying light danced across the thatched ceiling until the flames withered away. I lay back on the creaking charpai, cloaked in darkness. In the pitch-black hut, I couldn't tell whether my eyes were closed or open. I stared at nothing.

A piercing screech rent the air, entering the room and ricocheting off the walls. I sat up with a jolt and looked around me. For a while after, the only sound I heard was my own heartbeat. Then a deep-throated laugh echoed through the trees outside the hut.

I threw myself out of the charpai and rushed into the living space. It was empty save for the girl, who stood at the window, peering out. She turned her head and pressed a finger to her pursed lips.

We listened for another sound, but there was only the violent shaking of trees outside. I joined the girl at the window, looking out at the houses down the road and across the fields. Then, slowly, fires were lit, making the windows of houses burn like bright eyes. The village was waking up one hut at a time.

"She got another one."

The hair rose on the back of my neck. The girl didn't have to explain.

"Churailain don't exist."

I wondered for a moment if Naani had followed me to Kallikakundu, but for all of her witchiness, she was just a bitter old woman who missed her beti.

The girl snorted. "I didn't mention anything about a churail. If they don't exist, then why did you bring them up?" She headed back to her parents' room. "You'll see in the morning," she whispered, then disappeared inside.

I returned to bed, sweat dripping from my forehead, my heart thumping in the dark.

I squeezed my eyes shut, trying to force myself to sleep, but I couldn't latch onto a dream. I jumped off the charpai to pace the room when I heard a sharp knock on the front door. I froze, pressing myself against the wall. In the adjoining room, the ticket collector and his wife grumbled in their sleep. I imagined the girl lying awake as well, her heart pounding like my own.

Someone shuffled to the front door.

"Who's there?" the ticket collector called out.

I slid along the wall to listen to the voices outside. The thatched door scraped open, and a group of people speaking in muffled voices entered. There was a frightened gasp and something that sounded like an angry retort. Then the hut fell silent again. I waited for more, but the silence made my ears ring. I lay down on the charpai, holding my breath as the ropes under me groaned into place. Darkness pressed into me from all sides, and I fell into a feverish, dreamless sleep.

The house was quiet in the morning; the air smelled of eggs and ghee. I stepped out of my room, blinking at the bright white sunlight streaming in through the windows. The mother and girl sat on the ground quietly eating breakfast. The girl didn't seem to notice me when I joined them.

The mother laid a small scoop of egg on my plate. She sighed and looked out through the open door and muttered a prayer under her breath.

"Where is the ticket collector?" I asked.

"His name is Abdul," the girl offered in a soft voice. "And Ma is Fatima. You ought to know their names."

"Thank you," I said, but the girl wouldn't look at me.

"He's off to do a bit of work," Fatima Aunty replied. "He'll be home soon."

I took the few bites of my breakfast, chewing each rubbery morsel for a while but tasting nothing. I finished my meal, and Fatima Aunty insisted on washing the dishes, so I stepped outside and looked for my bicycle. It was nowhere in sight. I was sure I'd left it leaning against the house the night before. I ran around to the other side of the house to search for it. But it was gone.

"I'm sorry," the girl said, standing behind me with her hands clasped together. "Was it special to you?"

"It was," I choked, my voice on the edge of tears. The girl shushed me and pointed down the road. I spotted the ticket collector returning to his house, flanked by four men. Villagers who were out for a walk moved to the side of the road, and those sweeping their thresholds hurried back inside their huts to watch the five men pass with solemn eyes.

Abdul Uncle trudged past us without a word. He led the others into the house and shut the door.

The girl mumbled something and began walking down the road.

I followed close behind. "Is it true?"

The girl stopped to face me. "This whole time you've been in my house, you haven't asked me my name. Any of our names."

"Oh!" I stared at her upturned face. "What's your name?"

The girl drew herself up. "Shah Jehan Begum."

I laughed. "Did your parents think you should have been a boy?"

The girl narrowed her eyes. "No. That's my name. That's what they wanted to name me."

"King of the World," I said. "The name fits."

For the first time since I'd met her, Shah Jehan smiled at me. "Come here." She led me away from the hut to a dense cluster of trees past the road.

I hung back and peered into the wood. "Was it a . . . an actual . . ."

Shah Jehan touched the nearest tree. She sat down on its roots and patted a spot next to her. I sat down a few feet away from her, feeling a blush spread across my cheeks.

"It took a man," Shah Jehan said. "It always takes a man. And then my baba and his friends have to go and make it right again."

"I don't understand. I've never seen anything like this happen before."

"That doesn't mean it isn't real," Shah Jehan retorted. "A chur—"

"Don't say it." I could feel the goosebumps rising on my arms. "Please."

Hearing the leaves rustle, I glanced up at the branches above us and scooted closer to Shah Jehan. "Is that who is trying to starve you? Those creatures?"

Shah Jehan squinted at me. "No, that's something else entirely. I don't think you'd understand. You're not one of us."

"That's not fair."

"You city folk don't have what we have."

I looked around at flat plains painted in sandy browns and fertile greens, feeling closer to the earth than I'd ever felt before. Endless fields stretched out in front of us—rice paddies dotted with tiny twig-like bodies toiling in them.

"You're right," I said. "We don't."

She sat back, satisfied. "Tonight, there'll be a hunt. Want to join?"

At first, I thought I hadn't heard her right, but when Shah Jehan trained her striking eyes on me, I felt a rush of adrenaline coursing through my veins.

"But your papa said he'd take me to the train station."

"You can forget about that. The villagers have to bury a man today." Shah Jehan quickly turned away from me, but not before I'd noticed the tears in her eyes.

I reached out to touch her hand but withdrew at the last second.

"We know the family. When something like this happens in the village, it happens to all of us."

"But—" I began to speak. Shah Jehan turned to look at me.

"I need to go."

"There's something bigger here than the two of us, and the men in this village have taken it upon themselves to rid us of it. Are you coming or not?"

"Yes." I nodded without thinking.

"Don't worry." Shah Jehan stood and brushed the dirt off of her clothes. "Churails don't go after girls. I'll protect you."

Night fell too quickly. I stared out of the window and watched the sun hide behind a bank of clouds. Soon, the light from hurricane lanterns dotted the village.

Behind me, Abdul Uncle put an arm around his wife. "Stay inside. All of you. And Haroon," he said, beckoning me closer, "you'll take care of them while I'm gone?"

I didn't know what to say. Abdul Uncle smiled at me.

Together, we dragged a charpai from outside into the hut. I could feel Shah Jehan's dark eyes on the back of my head as I set it down in the middle of the room.

Abdul Uncle stood at the door and rubbed his chin, now sporting a salt-and-pepper stubble. He seemed to be aging in front of my eyes. Then, studying his family, he said, "I won't be long," and strode out of the hut to join a group of men assembled outside. Each man was armed with a rifle. Abdul Uncle was handed one, which he strapped on with practiced ease.

I watched them disappear down the road, then turned back to the inside of the hut.

"Well," Shah Jehan said aloud, "I'm ready for bed. You won't need to take care of me for the rest of the night." She headed for her room without looking back.

Fatima Aunty made her way to bed as well. "You should sleep. Who knows when they'll be home?" Her lower lip trembled as she stole one last glance at the door, then she hastened into her room.

I sat on my charpai and waited for a sign from Shah Jehan. Then, as the night wore on, I drifted off into a confused sleep, dreaming that I was back in my room, sleeping in my own bed in Cawnpore.

Something brushed my arm. My eyes shot open to see Shah Jehan's upside-down face above my head. I recoiled and backed away, but she covered my mouth with a hand.

"It's time," she whispered.

I rubbed the sleep from my eyes and followed her. We slipped through the back door, then crept around the side of the house. Somewhere in the village, wheels creaked, and a horse pawed the ground. We followed the sounds and found a cart standing idle beside a house.

"Come on!" Shah Jehan pulled herself up into the back of the cart.

The horse snorted and glared at us. Shah Jehan held her hand out for me. I took her hand, cool and soft despite the stifling humidity that rose in waves around me.

As I fell in beside her, I could hear the sounds of conversation floating over to us. Shah Jehan gasped, and I could feel her panicky heartbeat in the dark. We crawled on our knees, shoving aside sacks of wilted vegetables to settle under a rough blanket. As the voices neared, we rolled onto our stomachs under the blanket, our arms touching. I flushed, grateful it was too dark for her to see.

The wagon rocked as two men jumped on and took a seat on the sacks of rank-smelling vegetables in the back. Then we began to move, bumpily at first and then speeding up as the horse clip-clopped along.

Shah Jehan nudged me with a sharp elbow. "There's two in the back with us. My baba and another man are in the front."

"We shouldn't move around too much then," I whispered, afraid we would be caught.

I could feel her eyes on me in the darkness. Just then, the wagon swerved, sending me crashing into Shah Jehan.

"What was that?"

Shah Jehan peeked from under the blanket and sucked in her breath. Someone or something was right behind the wagon, their heavy footfalls thudding against the dirt road.

I tussled with the blanket to move it off my face, but Shah Jehan jerked it back. A screech tore through the night, sending the hair rising on my arms again. Shah Jehan slipped an arm around me and pulled me closer to her. The wagon clambered over the road, and I heard the distinct clack of rifles. The villagers cocked and loaded their guns for an enemy they couldn't see.

I moved the blanket off of one eye.

Two women galloped on all fours beside our wagon: their feet twisted backward, long braids swinging behind them, white saris rippling in the wind. A scream caught in my chest. I clutched my face, my mouth trying to form words.

We were being followed by a pair of churailain who hissed and kept pace with the wagon, their dead eyes staring at the rifles pointed at their hearts.

The wagon bumped over a pothole, and the blanket almost slipped off of us, but Shah Jehan kept a hold on it, hugging me with her other arm. One of the churailain lunged, using her legs to reach the edge of the wagon, her grizzled hand stretching to touch our blanket.

A gunshot rang out, and I yelped and covered my ears. The churail fell with a thump. She didn't rise again—her body melted into a black heap and dissolved into the earth.

The second churail continued her pursuit until another shot cracked through the whipping wind. It hit her in the arm, and she fell back a few paces. Then, as the wagon entered a dense stretch of wood and slowed down, she scrabbled up a tree, the wood splintering under her sharp fingernails.

The wagon came to a stop. There was a tinny ring in my ears: a phantom gunshot still lodged somewhere in my head. I couldn't stop shivering, and Shah Jehan rubbed my back to calm me.

She breathed against my ear, "It'll be okay. I'm sorry, I'm so sorry. Close your eyes. Don't watch."

But I could only stare, my tongue sloppy in my mouth, my stomach churning with sick. The riflemen jumped off the wagon along with Abdul Uncle. They approached the tree and stared up. A cackle rained down on them, and the branches creaked. Four men raised their rifles and aimed, but before they could shoot, the churail fell from the tree, pouncing on one of the men. She bent over his body and placed her mouth on his. Then, as his body writhed under her, his arms useless and beating the ground, she sucked the life out of him. What remained was a dry husk of a corpse.

Shah Jehan and I covered our heads with the blanket and held each other, our arms trembling. The churail hissed again, and several gunshots rang out. The scent of scorched earth wafted over to us.

The remaining hunters climbed aboard the wagon and drove back to the village. One of the men in the back of the wagon sobbed. "My brother," he moaned, beating the back of the wagon with his fists. "Take me home," he cried. "Take me home!"

The wagon traveled through the fields to the village and stopped outside a hut. We waited until the men disembarked and entered the newly deceased man's home. Then, Shah Jehan peeled the blanket off of us, wet now from our combined perspiration and agitated breaths, and helped me off the cart. As my feet touched the ground, I swayed on the spot, then bent over and vomited.

Shah Jehan patted my back as the meager morsels I'd eaten throughout the day came back up. "I was cruel to make you come with me."

I rubbed my runny nose with the back of my hand and wiped my tears on my sleeve, too sick to be embarrassed. "What if there are more of them?" I asked, catching my breath. I looked around us. "What if they're right here?"

Shah Jehan took my arm and led me away from the cart. "They don't live in villages like us. They live in the woods, in the trees."

"Only in this village."

"No, everywhere."

I shivered, aware of how warm Shah Jehan's arm was around me. "I've never seen anyone—anything—like this before."

"Maybe women are treated better in the cities then." Shah Jehan pulled me along. "We have to get home before my baba does," she said. "I'm sorry you're having a hard time believing what you saw, but it doesn't take me long to know what is real and what isn't."

We slipped through the village, quiet but for our soft footsteps, and hurried back to the hut. I glanced behind us, and once I was satisfied nothing had tracked us down, I followed Shah Jehan inside.

She led me to my charpai. "Goodnight," she whispered and went into her bedroom.

"Goodnight." I fell back onto the charpai. Cold sweat gathered on my forehead. I felt another wave of nausea rise, and I leaned over, thinking I'd be sick again, but the queasiness passed.

I was almost asleep when the front door rattled. I sat up and reached for the hurricane lamp at the foot of the charpai. It was Abdul Uncle. His gun was gone, his hunter stance replaced by his usual weary slouch. His eyes were bloodshot, and he blinked in the bright light of the hurricane lamp, then shut the door behind him.

He sat next to me on the charpai. "You shouldn't have done that. What if it saw you?"

"I don't know what you're talking about," I said.

Abdul Uncle gave me an exasperated look. "I know my daughter. She's fascinated with these things. I try to be stern like a good father should be with his daughter, but I have to let her be free to make her own decisions. What you saw out there could happen to my family."

I was nauseous again. "I don't know if what I saw was a nightmare or reality."

Abdul Uncle scratched his stubbly chin for the umpteenth time. "It's our reality. Maybe you are too young to understand the cruelty of our world."

I crossed my arms, not knowing how impetuous I must have looked. "I'm thirteen," I said. "I'm old enough to know."

Abdul Uncle's head nodded forward. He appeared to be thinking, then he shut his eyes and spoke. "When a woman dies an unnatural death, all the hate and bitterness is captured inside her heart. She then goes into the earth a human and rises a churail."

He added after a pause, "They never used to rise this often. Two nights in a row . . ."

I thought about Papa—Papa, who was out there somewhere, with his clean khaki uniform, starched the way I had last seen it. If he was in Burma, he was in the jungle. And the jungle was the nesting ground for those horrible creatures.

Despite the heat in the hut, I shuddered. "It's easy to treat women well," I said as I wrapped my arms around my middle. "I have seen my papa treat my ammi well."

Abdul Uncle grimaced. "The world doesn't always work that way, and it hasn't for a while. When you're older, you'll understand." He wiped the tears from his eyes and sighed, looking up at the roof. "Two burials in two days." He lumbered off the charpai and looked at me. "Get some sleep. We'll leave for the station early in the morning."

I awoke to a deafening silence. I could hear my heartbeat hammering in my ears as I lay on the charpai, my eyes adjusting to the light around me. I was in a stranger's home, a blanket of sadness smothering its occupants.

I could see Abdul Uncle standing outside the door in the early morning light, freshly shaved, wearing his work clothes, and holding a tiffin box filled with food. I tiptoed through the house to the washbasin and rinsed my face and arms. The water was cool and smelled of earth. I waited until the water dried before I headed outside, passing Shah Jehan's room. I contemplated waking her, telling her I'd be leaving soon to meet Papa, and that I might, well . . . I might miss her.

But I kept walking and joined Abdul Uncle outside, where the heady, intoxicating scent of cow manure and wet earth overwhelmed me. We walked along the road in silence. Solemn-looking villagers heading out to work in the fields nodded at Abdul Uncle as he passed. Chickens and cows steered clear of the road, seemingly aware that we had been close enough to touch something strange and terrifying, and they wanted nothing to do with us.

I mourned the loss of my bicycle. It had been a gift from Papa just before he'd gone off to the war front, and though I was already ashamed of myself for losing it, I knew Papa wouldn't ever chastise me. After all, what was losing a bicycle compared to losing my family to war?

I trailed some distance behind Abdul Uncle, a man who would soon become a stranger to me. I'd remember to speak highly of him once I reached Papa. And I'd write letters, every day if I had to, to thank him for his kindness. But as I opened my mouth to utter my thanks, my lips were dry, my tongue a parched brick. I found I'd lost my voice.

When we neared the train station, I felt the closest to Papa since I left home. I imagined I'd see Papa again in his heroic uniform, waiting for me at a train station. I stared down at my worn clothes, smudged with dirt from the wagon ride, hoping that when Papa saw me, he wouldn't mind my appearance. There were a million different ways I could start a conversation with him, and as my mind ran through the possibilities, the previous night's memories began to fade.

Abdul Uncle bought a ticket for me. "You should never steal to get on a train," he said with a tart wag of a finger. I took one last look around at the countryside with its lush fields and wet rice paddies. I knew that I would miss this place.

I snatched the ticket from Abdul Uncle and followed him into a compartment.

"I'll come back for you when your stop is near."

I squirmed in my seat, my feet tapping the ground in anticipation. The train lurched forward, picking up speed, and soon, I was whipped away from the past.

It wasn't long until Abdul Uncle entered the compartment, shouting, "Ticket, ticket!" When he approached me, I waved my ticket at him, and Abdul Uncle pocketed it with a smile.

Before I knew it, my eyes closed, my head nodded forward, and I was transported back to that dark wood. Except there was no wagon, no Shah Jehan. I wasn't alone. Two churailain circled me, with terrifying grins on their colorless faces.

They lunged at me at the same time, and I screamed, pushing their hands away as they tried to throttle me.

It was Abdul Uncle shaking me awake. "We've arrived," he said, without meeting my eyes.

We disembarked, and I followed Abdul Uncle into an oddly familiar-looking station. I searched for signs proving that I'd made it to Burma, anything to point me to Papa. Finally, I turned back, and Abdul Uncle was nowhere to be seen. The crowd parted, and Dr. Bannerji stepped forward, nervously crumpling his tie between his fingers. Behind Dr. Bannerji, a woman appeared. She was beautiful and sad and looked very familiar. Her eyes grew large when she spotted me, and she staggered back. Dr. Bannerji took hold of her arm.

It was Ammi, so thin and frail from the months of us being apart. She stretched out her arms, and I ran to her and threw my arms around her. She sobbed against me, her tears falling onto the back of my neck.

"I thought I'd lost you."

I pulled away from Ammi to glance at the train, but Abdul Uncle was gone. And so was Shah Jehan and the nightmare we'd shared.

Ammi gripped my hand in her own as a tonga took us back to Naani's house. "My beta went to Kallikakundu all by himself," Ammi whispered in awe. On my other side, Dr. Bannerji stared out at the road.

She pushed back the hair falling on my forehead. "You've been such a good boy taking care of your poor, sick Naani all this time."

It hadn't occurred to me that Naani was sick. Now, I recalled the nights spent lying awake listening to her coughs filtering through the walls. I washed the rust-colored stains from her sheets that I thought were paan juice from the betel leaves she chewed; I now realized it was blood, something much more serious.

Dr. Bannerji faced us. "Don't you think it's rather cruel to have left her alone?"

"Madhu," Ammi said in a stern voice, "you're a good friend of mine, but don't scold my son. He isn't yours to scold."

"I scold him because I care about him," Dr. Bannerji said. "It's a dangerous world out there. He's as precious as you are to me."

Ammi tut-tutted under her breath. Bannerji stared back at the city while Ammi held me close to her, hugging me so tight that I was almost afraid she'd spend the rest of her life embracing me, never letting go.

The tonga arrived outside Naani's house, and though I was too old to hold my mother's hand, I gripped Ammi's. She pulled me out after her and waved to Dr. Bannerji without looking at him. Behind us, the tonga sped off, and I imagined a somber, mournful-looking Bannerji looking back at us.

I let Ammi lead me back into the house. The house had a medicinal smell, and the furniture was coated in dust. I felt a twinge of regret at not having been around to clean it up.

Ammi spoke quietly to me. "I'm afraid Naani doesn't have much time left in the world."

My heart felt like it'd plunged into ice. "You said she was only sick." I was startled by the tears in my eyes.

"Her lungs—" Ammi began, then covered her face in her dupatta to dry her tears. "I haven't spoken to her since I married your papa. But then you vanished, and I got news that she became very sick. I thought—" Ammi began to cry. "When Muhammad told me he lost you in Calcutta, I said I'd never forgive him. But you've been safe all this time."

I didn't want to speak; harsh words bubbled up my throat. The hungry nights, the backbreaking labor, the constant reproach, and the complete lack of warmth from Naani. But I kept my silence and followed Ammi into Naani's bedroom. A doctor was at Naani's bedside, listening to her heart with a stethoscope. Ammi took a seat at Naani's side and patted her hand while I stood in the doorway. Naani's eyelids flickered, but she didn't open her eyes.

I approached the bed and gazed down at Naani. She opened her eyes and turned to stare up at her estranged daughter and grandson. I found she had aged: her black braid had more runs of gray, her lips wrinkled and sunken, no longer stained with paan. She wasn't a terrifying churail anymore, but an elderly, lonely woman. Her eyes glistened with tears as she smiled at me.

I smiled back at Naani, nodding to show that deep down, I knew I loved her and that I knew she loved me too. Then, as Ammi wept beside us, Naani shut her eyes and fell asleep.

# NINE

# THE FIGURE

Maera stepped in first. A blast of wet, humid air fogged her glasses, causing them to slip to the end of her nose. She took them off and gave them a hasty wipe with the hem of her shirt. The dirt path in front of her led into the dense, green interior of the greenhouse, seeming to go on endlessly. Vines dangled lazily from the trees, quivering eerily. Maera mopped the sweat from her forehead and glanced up at the thick tops of the trees. Through gaps in the leaves, she could see the sky churning with gray and green clouds.

Jimmy blinked away the sweat that was trickling into his eyes and pointed ahead.

"Peepal trees. Very interesting to see them in America."

"The glass walls are gone," Sara said, swatting away a vine that flapped around her head like a confused bird. "It just goes on and on in here."

"Should we follow the path?" Jimmy asked.

Leaves and gravel littered the start of the trail. Some distance ahead, the path was obscured entirely by plant life. Maera looked back at the entrance, then turned to the jungle in front of her, unsure.

"Let's do it," Rob said and pulled the door shut. It sealed itself with a vacuum pop.

"What are you doing?" Sara hissed as she shoved past him.

"I don't know. It made sense at the time."

Sara pushed her shoulder against the door, then turned back with a horrified look on her face.

"It's locked. We're locked in."

The heat unfurled around Maera like hot breath. Whatever they needed, it was right there inside, with them, whether the others understood it or not.

"We can worry about the door later." She didn't wait for a response.

Maera plunged in, the dirt crunching under her shoes. As Maera inched closer, the shrubs moved aside, revealing a trail veering off to the right. She stopped and waited for the figure to present itself again, but only the jungle whispered back, its foliage fluttering in the broiling wind.

Maera's forehead was damp, and she was sweating under her arms, behind her knees, and in the crevices of her elbows. Little trickles of perspiration traveled down her neck and dripped down her back.

Rob caught up with her, panting though they'd only traveled ten feet. "I also brought us a change of clothes."

He was soaked like he'd fallen into a deep body of water. A drop of sweat perched itself at the end of his eyelashes, and when he blinked, it burst into the air and was instantly absorbed by the air around them. Rob unzipped his backpack and dug inside. He tossed Maera a black tank top.

She held it out in front of her. "This is yours?"

Rob shrugged. "It's going to a good cause."

Maera stepped off the path and hid behind a tree. She peeked around to glance at Rob, whose face reddened. He spun on his heel and turned his back to her.

Maera's T-shirt was fused to her skin. As she peeled it off, the hot air touched her skin, cooling her off for a moment. She mopped her forehead with her shirt. Maera slipped the tank top on over her head, letting the dry shirt settle against her torso. It was too loose; her bra was visible through the arm holes. She twisted the shoulders into knots to make the top fit her snugly. She now smelled like laundry detergent mixed in with the faint musk of boy. Maera flushed as she heard the gravel skitter behind her as Sara and Jimmy caught up to Rob. She ignored the butterflies in her stomach to join the others.

Sara gave her a once-over. "Okay, what? What is this?"

"It was hot," Maera said. "I was completely soaked. I can breathe now."

Jimmy gave Maera an appreciative smile. "You look like Rambo."

Rob stripped off his shirt. Maera glanced away, but the corners of her eyes strained overtime to get a glimpse of his gleaming torso. He slipped on an identical tank top. Maera finally exhaled as the T-shirt settled around his hips.

"There's more if you guys want to change," Rob said.

Sweat rings soaked Jimmy's and Sara's collars, and the damp spread out around their armpits, but before Jimmy could say anything, Sara put up her hand. "No, thanks."

The tree branches creaked above; the boughs seemed to brandish their fists at them. A few leaves fluttered to the ground, and Maera was back in The Past, to Naana's house, to the one time she dared sneak into the back garden. She'd had just enough courage to place one foot outside and watch a downpour clear the perpetual dust from the air and dribble down the sloping sides of the greenhouse. The leaves had littered the ground, and she had been awash in that same cool green smell that surrounded her now.

Rob glanced at Maera and gestured toward the path. "After you."

After they rounded a curve, Sara kept pace with Maera, gasping in the humid atmosphere. "I don't like this," Sara said. "This doesn't feel right. I have goosebumps, and it's a thousand degrees in here. I need to document this," Sara pulled her phone out of her pocket. She held the phone out in front of her, turned the video camera on, and pressed record. The seconds ticked by as Sara captured the greenery and the tangle of vines above their heads. Maera rubbed the back of her neck and discreetly glanced behind her. Rob was speaking to Jimmy, and Jimmy murmured in reply.

Sara spun her camera around to focus on Rob and Jimmy, walking backward to keep pace with Maera.

"There's nothing here," Sara said, finally. She stopped recording and put her phone in her pocket. "Just trees and green stuff and hot air."

"That's not true," Maera said. "I think I saw something earlier tonight."

Sara narrowed her eyes at Maera. "What exactly was this something?"

Maera pushed the soggy strands of hair off her forehead. "It was a person. I think."

Sara blocked Maera's path. "You're telling me you saw someone, and now we're locked in here with some . . . thing?"

"Not something." Maera wasn't entirely sure.

Hearing a sudden rustling, Sara gripped Maera's arm, her nails digging unpleasant crescent-moon shapes into Maera's skin. The trees groaned as the wind picked up, the fallen leaves swirling around them like they were caught in a funnel.

Maera found they had reached a fork in the road.

"Woah. The trail has changed."

The four of them unconsciously moved into a huddle. They were facing a gnarled, two-headed tree that snaked its way upward. The main trail diverged into two around the roots of the tree.

Maera looked down each trail, then behind her, but the path they'd arrived on didn't look any different from the ones ahead.

"I have an idea." She held her hand out to Rob. "I saw a ball of twine in your bag."

Rob rummaged in his backpack and produced the ball of twine Maera had seen earlier. As she took it from Rob's outstretched hand, their fingers brushed. A lone butterfly tickled her insides, and Maera snatched the twine with both hands to steady herself.

"We'll tie the string around the tree and then split up into pairs. Each pair can take one end of the twine. We can go as far as it'll unspool, and if anything happens, we'll backtrack and meet at this spot."

Maera used a loose piece of twine to tie the spool to the tree. She pinched her fingers and began pulling out the string. She held one end clasped in one hand and handed the other to Jimmy.

"I'll go with him," Sara said and slid closer to Jimmy, who was staring at the ground and rubbing his arm.

Rob stood at Maera's side. "Guess I'm with you."

Maera held her end of the string tight and moved from one agitated foot to the other. "Let's give ourselves fifteen minutes. If you reach a dead-end, come back and meet us at the tree. If we don't see anything at all, we'll come back here and regroup."

Jimmy wrapped the twine around his hand several times and nodded to Maera. She gave him a small encouraging smile and hoped he'd smile in return, but he tugged at the twine all business-like.

Beside him, Sara shivered despite the heat. "I hope it doesn't change around us again."

"We'll still have this." Maera held up the string. "It can't change what we brought in from outside."

"You think so?" Jimmy asked.

Maera shrugged. "Let's work with what we got. We have fifteen minutes."

She set a timer on her phone for fifteen and watched as Sara did the same.

"See you on the other side?" Maera tried to sound encouraging, but Sara didn't reply. Instead, she pocketed her phone and took Jimmy's arm, and spun him around toward their path. Soon, the greenery swallowed them whole.

Maera turned back to her trail. The twine fell slack and tightened as she pulled it onward to keep pace with Rob. He was walking so close to her that Maera felt his hand brushing her own more than once. They were alone again. This time, she fell mute, her mouth suddenly dry.

Rob cleared his throat and gave her a sidelong glance. "You know, all this time, I've been right next door to you."

She stifled a sigh. "I want to say I didn't forget about you—"

"But you forgot about me," Rob said, and Maera heard a sheepish smile in his voice.

"But you stayed," Maera said. "Of all the colleges you could have chosen, you chose Georgetown."

Rob stared at the ground. He kicked the pebbles off the trail in front of him and shoved his hands into his pockets.

"A part of me didn't want to leave. I wanted to stay close because of him. Like going somewhere far away would create distance between me and my memories of him. Even when it destroyed me that you guys went from being my second family to complete strangers. I had to trespass to get your attention again."

Maera flushed, feeling the heat creep up her neck and onto her cheeks. She conjured up that memory of Rob again, that fleeing glance as the door slammed shut. They'd lost so many years, so much time they could have spent consoling each other, moving on together.

Maera wanted to take his hand but couldn't find the will to do it. "You got my attention now. What do I do to make it up to you?"

They stopped before a gnarled branch obstructing their path. Before Maera could move, Rob bounded forward and dragged it off the trail, shoving it with his foot onto the grass beside them. "Why don't I tell you later," he said as he rejoined her on the trail, and she felt that flutter in her chest again.

"You can tell me now." Maera swung around to face him. "We're, um, alone."

But Rob didn't seem to hear her. He looked down at his hands and brushed the dust off his palms. "A dead tree is usually teeming with bugs. There was nothing there. It's just all this." He waved at the foliage around them. "Just trees and vegetation. No signs of human or insect life."

Maera coughed. "Don't be so sure. I thought I saw someone in here."

"You what?" Rob held up a hand to stop Maera from responding. "You should've said something. I told you this place could be dangerous."

Maera drew closer to him and lowered her voice, even if it was just the two of them on the trail. "All of us—all of us—have been thinking about Asad since this thing appeared. I'm just drowning in memories of him. I know you are too."

"You knew something else was in here and didn't mention it and brought us in with you?" Rob's shoulders tensed as he balled up his hands. Maera wasn't sure if he was livid or that he expected something to come out of the grass to attack them.

"It's because he's here," she gestured to the trees around them, "he's here."

Rob shook his head. "You can't do this to us. Leading us in here because you think your dead brother—"

Maera's face grew hot. She turned back to the trail and stomped onward, leaving Rob several feet behind. She was so focused on the trees ahead that she missed seeing a large rock in her way. She tripped and stumbled onto the ground as the stone rolled past her into the grass.

Rob jogged up to her. "Are you okay?"

Maera nodded, too red-faced to look at him, and rubbed the toe that had smashed against the rock. Rob bent to pick up the stone. As he brought it closer, Maera realized what it was. She felt the greenhouse tilting as the ground beneath her careened sideways.

"Give it here."

Rob dropped it into her outstretched palm. It was a miniature horse carved out of wood, encrusted in mud.

Tears blurred the outline of the toy in her hand. "I knew it. I knew it was him."

Maera turned the toy over, scratching the dirt off with her fingernails, and looked at Rob. "This is Asad's. My dad used to make these for him." Maera pushed herself up and hugged the toy to her chest. "He's been here. All these years, he's been here."

A sudden fierce wind picked up around them. Rob said something, but the whipping air drowned out his voice. The wind appeared to throttle the bushes on either side of the trail, and above them, the trees shook their spinsterish heads.

Maera picked up the string she had dropped when she fell to the ground. It trembled in her hand for a second, and then someone snatched it away. "Ow!" Maera opened her palm to find a red slash across it.

Rob took off after their end of the string. "Wait!" Maera called out but couldn't even hear herself. The darkness swallowed up Rob.

A high-pitched screech ripped through the air. Maera froze, and then a sudden burst of adrenaline sent her running along the path, further into the foliage, the leaves scratching at her arms and legs. An animal was chasing her. It smelled of blood and earth and something frighteningly familiar. She turned her head to see, but she could only hear the sound of pounding feet and a dry, hollow panting.

Maera tripped and fell, scraping her elbows. Almost immediately, vines curled out of the ground and stroked her arms. She slapped them away and struggled back onto her feet. The jungle was closing in on her. Maera turned around in circles. Her tank top was soaked and clung to her body, and she struggled to catch her breath. The wind faltered, then fell away. Finally, the jungle quieted, her ragged breathing the only sound in the dark.

The leaves in front of her parted, and a woman emerged. She was crawling on all fours, feeling her way across the ground. She was slowly closing the gap between her and Maera, who had backed up against a withered tree trunk. The woman had a misshapen mouth revealing long teeth, glinting in the low light. She gazed at Maera, her face weathered and stretched, her long dark hair a mess of tangles.

The ground hissed as she neared. Maera followed the length of hair to look at the woman's feet, which were twisted backward and capped with dagger-like toenails.

Maera filled her lungs to scream, but she couldn't make a sound. She pressed her back into the trunk, her legs trembling. The creature stopped crawling and rose to a height of nearly seven feet, her features suddenly transforming into the face of a calm, untroubled woman. The wild hair fell tamely to her shoulders, untangled itself, and swiveled into a thick braid. A white sari settled around her frame and swished against her backward-facing feet.

"That's better," she said and smirked at Maera.

This time Maera managed to scream, and the flora to her left rustled. Jimmy jumped out to shield her from the creature. It bared its fangs and hissed at them. Jimmy yanked Maera, and they ran, crashing through the foliage till they bumped right into Rob and Sara. Another piercing scream rang out behind them. The four of them took off down the trail, the hanging vines whipping their faces and snaking around their wrists to take hold of them. Finally, they arrived at the two-headed tree and veered right, running back down the original trail. The door appeared through the foliage. Maera surged forward and crashed into the door. It sprang open with little effort, and they toppled out onto the grass. As they lay panting, they felt the mild summer air whirl around them, cooling them off.

Maera sat up and peered into the greenhouse. The woman stood in the trees, arms to her side. Her dark red eyes stared back for a moment, and then the door slammed shut with a loud crack.

# TEN

# THE MOTHERS

Maera got to her feet and faced the others, but they were still on the ground, crawling back from the greenhouse. "Get away from that thing," Sara shrieked, but Maera stayed put in front of the door.

"I knew it." Maera paced feverishly.

Jimmy reached out. "Get away from there."

Maera clenched her fists. "I'm not moving from this spot. Asad is in there, and that thing has him."

Sara gasped. "He can't have been in there all this time."

Rob ran a hand through his hair and threw a wild look toward the greenhouse door. "What was . . . what just tried to attack us?"

"It was a churail," Jimmy said, staring ahead with a clenched jaw.

The four of them turned their heads at the same time to face the greenhouse. An eerie light swirled inside, pulsing to a phantom heartbeat. Maera and Sara shared a wide-eyed look while Rob glanced at the others in turn.

"What the hell is a churail?" he asked.

"It's a witch." Sara shivered. Her teeth began to chatter, and she rubbed her arms to warm herself.

Jimmy gave a solemn shake of his head. "Not a witch, a churail. A witch casts spells and makes potions and things like that. A churail is a bloodsucking demon that targets men."

"Like a succubus?" Rob asked. "I'm still not following. Did your grandfather have something to do with this?"

"It's in Naana's journal," Jimmy said. "He said he saw a churail in the jungle when he was young, somewhere in Bengal. He wrote that he was terrified of them."

"Then why does his greenhouse have a churail inside?" Rob asked.

They stared at one another.

"He captured her," Maera said. "And then she stole Asad from us when we were in Pakistan."

"It's impossible," Jimmy said as Sara helped him to his feet. "All of this is impossible."

"Is it?" Maera tossed Jimmy the toy horse she'd slipped into her pocket.

It took him a moment to realize what it was. He inspected it in his hands and rubbed it against his palm to get the dirt off. "He had this toy with him in Pakistan. I still remember him playing with it."

"I remember those things, too," Rob said as Jimmy tossed it to him. "He took them everywhere with him. I think this one was his favorite."

Maera pointed at the greenhouse. "That thing has him. It took him from us." She headed back to the greenhouse door, ignoring the gasps behind her. She could see the churail lurking among the trees, watching them from the inside.

"Yoohoo!" Maera hollered, followed by a nervous, high-pitched laugh.

"Maybe you shouldn't be taunting it," Rob warned, but Maera ignored him. Her body trembled, nervous energy still pulsing through her.

"Come out!" She slapped at the glass. The creature stepped back and disappeared from view.

"Ha!" Maera turned around. "She went and hid from me. The whole time this thing was here, not once did she come out to attack us." Maera glanced at Jimmy and realized he'd been clutching the diary in his hands. "We need to know more about churailain. We need to find out how to bring Asad home."

Somewhere above them, lightning flashed deep in the clouds. The greenhouse mimicked the sky, burning and blinking at the same time. Maera felt a chill surge through her spine and turned her back on the greenhouse.

"Keep watch," she said to Rob, who reached into his backpack and dug out a hammer. It glinted in the dark as he placed himself in front of the door.

Jimmy held the diary tight and didn't move to open it. "Just because his toy was in there, it doesn't mean—"

Maera didn't wait for him to finish. Instead, she walked toward the house.

"Wait!" Jimmy urged, but Maera kept going.

"Where are you going?" Sara called out to Maera. "Shouldn't we talk about this?"

Maera slid through the patio door and entered the kitchen. She could feel her heart beat in a frenzied rhythm, and she leaned against the wall to catch her breath. Sweat trickled down from her temples, mingling with the tears streaming down her face. Maera shut her eyes for a moment.

"I knew it," she said to herself and stifled a sob. As her heart rate slowed, the comedown left her lightheaded. She brushed away the tears and crept to the living room. The mothers were awake; Maera could hear their tense voices floating into the kitchen. She held onto the doorframe and listened, trying to discern the two similar-sounding voices. It was Ammi's she heard first.

"We had no claim on it, and I don't want it anyways." Her voice was hoarse, and Maera knew it was because she'd been crying.

"If we sold it, it would help us, especially you," Aisha Khala said. "If I call Muhammad Chacha right now, he would understand."

"How well did that work for me ten years ago?" Ammi asked. "When I uprooted my family to stay in that house." She almost spat out the word.

"Without a man's income—"

"You don't have one either," Ammi retorted.

Aisha Khala sighed. "How much longer are you going to struggle as a single mother? What's going to happen when your daughter eventually leaves home?"

Her temples pounding, Maera waited until Ammi spoke again. "Maera won't leave. She wouldn't do that to me."

Maera stopped herself from running right out into the room to tear up the place, to scream, to beg her mother to open her mind. Instead, she rested her cheek against the cool wall as she listened to Aisha Khala grunt as she sat down on the sofa in the living room. The springs in the couch compressed with a twang.

"I'm sure Maera doesn't want to be stuck in Grey Gardens with you for the rest of her life," Aisha Khala said. When Ammi didn't respond, Aisha Khala let out a long laugh. "You've never heard of Grey Gardens? No wonder."

The springs creaked again as Ammi joined her sister on the couch. "Look at us arguing with each other. Both single. One kid each. As if we were allowed to fall in love and lose them too. Our father cursed us."

They fell silent, and Maera took that moment to peek into the living room. Ammi and Aisha Khala sat next to each other, holding hands. They looked up at the same time when she entered.

"What are you wearing?" Ammi asked.

Maera looked down and realized she was still wearing Rob's tank top. She crossed her arms over her chest. "I borrowed it from Sara. It was hot outside."

Aisha Khala raised an eyebrow. "That looks large for Sara."

"I need to tell you something. Something's happened." The tears were back, pushing up against her lower lids like a gathering storm. She couldn't remember the last time she cried in front of her mother.

Ammi sensed her anguish and reached for her. "Where are the others? What's happened?"

"We're okay," Jimmy said as he entered the living room.

He leaned against the wall and stared at Maera. She turned her back on him.

"It's Asad," she said.

The color drained from Ammi's face. She squeezed her hands together as if begging Maera not to bring up The Past.

"We have been thinking about him," Jimmy said. "That's all."

Maera felt his eyes on the back of her head. "It's not that," she tried to explain, but she felt like she had disappeared from the room because the mothers stared past her toward Jimmy.

"Did you sort out the will?" Jimmy asked.

Ammi relaxed and sat back. "You can tell them," she said to Aisha Khala. "I suppose they're old enough to know these things by now."

"Well, beta," Aisha Khala said, settling into the couch, "we got a call from our cousins in Karachi. It seems like our abbu left us nothing and nothing for you kids either. The house belongs to his only living brother, who's so old he can't make any decisions. But who are we to be greedy?" Aisha Khala glanced at Ammi. "Now's not the time for such things."

"He did leave you something," Maera said. "The greenhouse. In the backyard."

Ammi shook her head and pinched the bridge of her nose. "Not right now."

"You know, the greenhouse that sprang up out of nowhere? The one with the churail in it?"

Aisha Khala snorted. "A churail? Really?"

Maera stood her ground, fists planted on her hips.

"Did your churail have a long black braid and a scary face?" Aisha Khala asked. "Were her feet turned backward?"

"Yes, and she talked to me." Maera grew hot.

Ammi wouldn't look at her. "See," she said to Aisha Khala, "even from beyond the grave, he's tearing my family apart."

Aisha Khala yawned. "This jet lag. We're all tired and need to get some sleep. Look at your eyes," she said to Ammi and tsk-tsked. She stood up and pulled Ammi up with her.

Maera threw up her hands. "It's pointless," she said to Jimmy as they watched the mothers stumble off to bed.

Once the mothers left the room, Maera looked for Asad's and her old sleeping bags in the basement. Jimmy watched her from the doorway as she rooted around in the linen closet.

"Why didn't you back me up in there?" Maera demanded to know as she threw aside duvet covers and fitted sheets. "You derailed everything."

Jimmy bent down to help Maera pull out the sleeping bags. "It seems you should back yourself up."

"What's that supposed to mean?" Maera asked, digging under a pile of wilted pillow cases. "Something is getting lost in translation over here."

"You're going to college soon. You should talk to your mom before it's too late. Before it gets more uncomfortable for you." Jimmy hauled up a sleeping bag.

"You don't know anything about that," Maera said.

Jimmy shifted the bundle in his arms. "Sara told me. You are very upset, but you haven't tried to talk to her yet."

"Did Sara also tell you that I'm going to talk to my mom whenever I feel like it? Right now, I don't feel like it. Right now, there are a lot more pressing concerns like, I don't know, a magical mystery greenhouse in my backyard?"

Jimmy turned away and started for the stairs.

"Can you back me up next time?" Maera called out, but Jimmy didn't respond.

Maera followed Jimmy to the backyard, where they found Rob unzipping his sleeping bag. Sara sat apart from him, wrapped in a large warm blanket, typing frantically on her phone. They arranged themselves in front of the greenhouse, facing the door.

Thick clouds blotted out the stars. Above them, the sky flashed with lightning; the greenhouse blinked in tandem. "Did you guys see that?" Maera asked, but the others didn't hear her. She waited for the approaching wave of thunder above her, but the clouds continued rolling by.

"You really think he's in there?" Sara asked, slipping her phone into the mass of blankets.

"We shouldn't claim anything without evidence," Jimmy cut in.

The sky and greenhouse flashed again, almost like a taunt, and Maera felt her cheeks burn.

"We found his toy," Maera said. "And he went missing at Naana's house. There was no way he could have gotten out of the house on his own."

"Or maybe he went in once and lost his toy. Just because it was in there doesn't mean he's still in there. Or that he's still alive," Jimmy said quietly.

"Come on, man," Rob said. "I haven't stopped thinking about him since this thing appeared. I know you can feel it too."

Jimmy looked sullen. He rubbed his face until his cheeks were pink. "I can too, but I don't want to get my hopes up. None of us should." He slithered into his sleeping bag. "We have to go through the churail first."

"We'll sleep in turns," Rob said, glancing at Maera for approval. She nodded, and Rob turned back to the others.

"If anything happens, in case it manages to find a way out, we have these." An odd assortment of weapons was laid out in front of them—several pairs of scissors, a hedge trimmer, knitting needles, a box cutter, and the hammer Rob had brought with him.

"And we can't let it get away without first finding out where Asad went." Maera zipped up the sleeping bag and slipped inside, fighting off the urge to fall asleep right away.

Beside her, Sara lay on her back and stared up at the sky. "Churailain have a Wikipedia page," she whispered.

Sara wormed closer to Maera. "Churailain like trees; they can live in forests or the mountains. They can change shape."

Maera shivered and wrapped her arms around herself, but the cold snuck into the sleeping bag and stayed with her. "That's what she did," Maera said. "She came out of the trees crawling on all fours. Then she stood upright like a woman."

Jimmy thumbed through the pages to find one he'd folded over. Maera noticed several folded edges and wondered how much Jimmy had managed to read. As Jimmy flicked through the diary, Maera watched the greenhouse dim with every turn of the page as if it were keenly hanging onto their conversation.

Jimmy turned his head away from the pages. "He wrote of churailain in detail. Bits and pieces are scattered throughout this book. Like pages of an encyclopedia.

"Naana says they are born from extreme violence and horror," Jimmy continued. "Maybe years ago, something terrible happened to the woman that created this churail. Churailain seek revenge on those they think wronged them. But only men."

Maera sat up, still encased in the sleeping bag, arms crossed over her chest like Ammi. "What about boys? Specifically, nine-year-old boys?"

Jimmy stared at the diary. "I'm not sure."

"It has to be in there," Maera said. The greenhouse glared at Maera with its obtrusive eye. "There's no way someone could have gotten into my grandfather's house in the middle of the night and taken my brother without anyone hearing a thing. Besides," Maera freed her hands and touched the ground beside her, crumbling a few blades of grass between her fingers as she reminisced, "there never was a body. We searched and searched and found no sign of him."

Sara reached out to touch Maera's shoulder. "How do we destroy it?" she then asked Jimmy.

Jimmy turned a few pages and frowned. Maera spotted a folded-up note stuck between two pages. Before she could reach for it, Jimmy had it in his hands and opened it with careful fingers.

"What is that?" Rob asked.

Maera was able to see enough to know what it was. "It's a letter. Read it aloud."

Jimmy sat in silence, his eyes running over the words, then cleared his throat to translate it for them. "Dear King of the World, I believe this might be the third letter I've written that will go unanswered. Have I angered you? Upset you? Calcutta is sopping wet and dreary, more so because Naani passed last night. I am sad, but I'm also not sad, if that makes sense. I don't know what it's like to have someone I used to know die, because I still feel her presence all around us. Ammi is awfully stressed. We had to bury Naani within twenty-four hours—and on top of all that, settle 'her affairs'. What do you think that means?

"Have I upset you or annoyed you? Will you come to visit me? Ammi said we wouldn't stay here for long. She wants to go back to U.P. right away. But I still want to see Papa. Ammi won't even let me ask about it. She tightens her lips and ignores me when I mention it.

"I hope I haven't upset you, King of the World. It would be nice to hear from you again." Jimmy folded up the letter.

"Who is the 'King of the World' he keeps mentioning?" Sara asked.

"It's her," Jimmy said, flipping through the diary until he landed on a page with a drawing of a shabby-looking tent, with a girl sitting behind its folds and looking out. Even with the rough outlines, Maera could tell the girl had a striking pair of eyes. She would have been much more beautiful than what her naana had managed to capture.

She had an urge to grab the diary from Jimmy, but Maera controlled herself.

"Fill them in."

They listened as Jimmy pieced together what they knew of his and Maera's naana—how he'd run away from home to try to find his father in Burma and how he met a girl in Bengal along the way.

"That's so sweet," Sara said with a dreamy smile. "He had a girlfriend."

Jimmy turned back to the beginning of the diary. "I don't know about that yet," he said. "This diary is out of order. I'm still figuring out the beginning, middle, and end of this story." Jimmy set the book down and rubbed his eyes, and turned over in his sleeping bag.

"Sara and Jimmy, you both sleep first," Maera said as Sara bundled herself in the blankets, her eyes already half-closed.

Rob sat hunched over, eyeing the greenhouse. Soon, his eyes began to close, and he jerked awake.

"Why don't you shut your eyes for a while? I'll wake you if anything happens," Maera whispered.

Rob shook his head. "I'm good."

Maera smiled at him. "I'll be fine."

Rob yawned and lay back into his sleeping bag.

Within moments, he was asleep. Maera watched the others doze, following the slow rise and fall of their chests, until the night deepened around them. She unzipped her sleeping bag. From their haphazard arsenal, she picked a pair of scissors and slipped them into her back pocket and carried the hammer in one hand.

Maera jiggled the handle, but the door was locked. The greenhouse blasted Maera with a beam of brilliant light, like a scream. She watched as the greenery danced to the whims of a caged wind. Beyond, the churail stood in the shadows, red eyes trained in her direction.

"I'm not afraid of you," Maera whispered. "Let me in."

The lock clicked and the handle depressed in her hand. Maera opened the door with a glance behind her. The others lay in a deep sleep, shrouded in darkness.

Maera shut the greenhouse door behind her.

# ELEVEN

# THE LETTER

Calcutta, India, 1943

After the monsoon came, beating down against the shutters, transforming the back garden into a swamp, Naani finally fell into an eternal sleep. Ammi sat at her bedside and wept day and night, but I chose to stay in my room, even after the funeral, composing yet another letter to Shah Jehan.

"Dear friend," I wrote, then scratched out the words and began again. "Dear Shah Jehan . . . "

Once I'd written another letter I was sure was going to go unanswered, I went looking for an envelope, but I was soon distracted by terse voices streaming up from Ammi's room below me. Her soft lyrical tones clashed with a man's clumsy bass. I hurried out of my room and raced down the stairs but stopped midway when I realized it wasn't Papa's voice I had heard. After all, I couldn't recall a time they'd raised their voices at one another. It was always Ammi who had the upper hand; she'd talk first, and Papa would listen with rapturous silence. Then he'd make a joke and break her concentration, and they'd laugh and laugh.

This time, the voices rose like waves and crashed against one another. "You don't understand. There is a right side and a wrong side. You're on the wrong side."

"Stop this nonsense. I can't hear it anymore," Ammi said.

"While you hide in your mother's beautiful house, they starve. They can't afford the most basic human need: food, to be able to afford sustenance." A pair of feet paced against the rug. When the scraping quieted, I recognized the voice.

Dr. Banerji. He spoke softly, "They're dying out there. Their bodies lay scattered on the streets, eaten by jackals."

"I—I didn't know there was a famine," Ammi said so quietly that I almost didn't catch her words.

"Because they hide the truth from us. It's just as Bose-ji said. I've been telling you something like this was bound to happen."

"Your Bose-ji is the one on the wrong side," Ammi said, her voice muddled with tears. "We're fighting for freedom, and not just our own. Don't forget that."

Bannerji let out an exasperated sigh. "The Empire doesn't give a damn what you're fighting for. Our own people are starving to death, and they burn our fields and send what's left to their precious soldiers."

"My husband and children are those precious soldiers."

I stepped off the last stair and moved closer to the door, a film of sweat forming on my forehead.

"I've had enough," Ammi said.

I took a step back, waiting for my heart to quiet its wild beating.

Bannerji's voice trembled, heavy with tears. "We're trapped here. Our freedom doesn't matter whether they win or lose this war."

"I told you to leave."

"They treat us like savages," Bannerji said, his voice rising. "You refuse to see it. Because you Muslims are the elites to them, and we Hindus their heathen boogeymen."

I took in a rattling breath as my mind spun. The country I thought I knew was a grownup's plaything, a toy that they passed back and forth until it crumbled into pieces in their rough palms.

"Come with me," Bannerji said suddenly. "You and your son. We'll leave the country. We'll move across the border."

"I'll wait for my husband in our own home."

"Rukhsana."

The weight of Ammi's name on Bannerji's lips brought the world around me to a standstill.

"I've always loved you. Even if you didn't choose me, I'll still always love you."

I gripped the wall with sweaty palms.

Then it was Ammi again. "Go fight for your cause, and we'll fight for ours."

The door flew open. I backed away from the room, but I was still in view when Dr. Bannerji staggered out with a tear-stained face. When he spotted me, his face softened. He wiped his tears with the back of his hand, then pulled out a folded piece of paper from his pocket.

"Good luck."

"You're leaving us to fight in the war, just like Papa," I said.

Bannerji shook his head. "Not the war you're thinking of." He glanced back at Ammi's room, handed me the note, and then strode out of the house.

I ran to the window and watched Dr. Bannerji take quick steps down the street until he turned a corner. He was gone. Behind me, Ammi shut her door in a fit of sobs, but she'd already wept so much since Papa and the twins left, her tears no longer had any effect on me.

I unfolded the paper in my hand. It was a colorful flyer with drawings of Indian soldiers, their bodies bound by shackles as they fired at an unseen enemy. A scowling, rotund man held their chains; a Union Jack was prominently displayed on his paunch. Words in English, Hindi, and Bengali read: "Indian warriors. You long to be free! We East Asian races are racing toward freedom. Thousands of your soldiers have already joined the Japanese Army. We shall defeat the enemy together!"

I looked back out of the window and up at the sky, remembering the planes that dropped the bombs over the city. Would those same planes soon pick Dr. Bannerji up to fight Papa in the jungle?

# TWELVE

# THE HUNGER

Bengal, India, 1943

Shah Jehan stared out of the window at the villagers shuffling past their broken homes. The loss of fat and muscle degradation had elongated their limbs; they looked like living brown skeletons. It used to seem so sudden—the starvation hitting each home like a quick-moving virus, but the horror of it had worn off by the time the affliction took her own family.

She missed Baba. Baba was away, as usual, helping others when they needed it most. He'd gone to bury another family: a father who had shot his children, his wife, and then turned the gun on himself to stave off the terror of succumbing to starvation. With no strength left to carry the corpses, Baba and the other volunteers had to tie ropes to the bodies and drag them through the mud to a makeshift cemetery.

Shah Jehan sat in a daze. With nothing left to do, she'd spent the morning crying while Ma lay on the charpai beside her, unable to move. Then, finally, when she had no energy left for tears, Shah Jehan stared out at the world and hoped that when she blinked, the world would right itself again, and her friends would reappear.

Abeera. Beautiful Abeera. She was the favorite of all her friends. Such long, thick hair, and soft, round features. Like Shah Jehan's family, Abeera's parents had sold their utensils, their furniture, anything they could find to have enough annas to pay for a fistful of rice.

Shah Jehan stared down at her distended stomach, then at her weak legs. Alarmed, she realized she looked like the dehydrated corpse that remained after churailain sucked a body dry. And where had they gone? Was Kallikakundu now undesirable to them, not worth haunting anymore? Or had the churailain been replaced with something else, something far more dangerous than those supernatural beings?

It wouldn't be long now. Someone would tie a rope and drag their bodies through the mud to their final resting places. Or . . . Shah Jehan was worth more to her family alive than dead. When they had run out of things, Abeera's family had sold something far more precious than metal. And before her parents took to such desperate measures . . . Shah Jehan held onto the careening world and stood up.

Ma stirred and held out a weak hand to Shah Jehan.

"We're leaving," Shah Jehan said. "We're leaving, and I know a place we can go to." She staggered to the charpai and pulled up Ma's limp body, her arms trembling. Ma sat up, leaning her frail body against Shah Jehan.

Baba shuffled in through the door, wearing only a dhoti and wiping the sweat and tears from his face. His ribs poked through a thin layer of skin, and he groaned as he breathed in and out. At the sight of their determined faces, he stumbled in

146

and threw his sinewy arms around his family. "What's happened?" he asked.

"We have to go," Shah Jehan said. "If we don't, we'll die here."

Baba's arms fell slack. He stared at the floor in resignation.

"We will follow you." A single tear trickled down his sunken cheek and fanned out to mingle with sweat.

# THIRTEEN

# THE GOODBYE

Calcutta, India, 1943

I walked the streets of Calcutta, periodically looking up at the sky. The city was transforming day by day. Before, I could stick my tongue out and taste the salt in the air; now, it was the rusty tang of gunmetal and war. Soldiers streamed into the city, taking over Chowringhee Road, filling up The Grand Hotel, and pouring in and out of the shops. They roared by in jeeps on the way to nightclubs, whooping and throwing money at us pedestrians.

I spotted a group of soldiers on their way to the Maidan, with two brown boys scurrying after them, carrying burlap bags. "Hai!" I shouted and hurried after them.

As I neared the group, I grabbed one of the boys by his shoulder and turned him around. The boy's bag fell to the ground. He scowled up at me. "What do you want? Can't you see I'm working?"

"Oi, blackie!"

A tall British soldier strode over to us. He stared at us as his boy hauled up his bag. "And you filthy wog," the soldier added, turning to me. "You leave our errand boys alone."

With a sudden crack, the soldier slapped me across the face. I stumbled to the ground, angry tears stinging my eyes.

The soldier towered over me. "Don't you speak English?"

I glared up at the man. "I do," I replied in English. "And my wog father is fighting for your country."

A dark-haired soldier shoved the man aside and stood between us while the errand boys scattered from the scene. The British soldier spat on the ground and walked away, whistling to his boy to follow him.

The sun blazing down on me made the heat of embarrassment I was feeling even more intolerable. I looked up at the dark-haired soldier's uniform. It had a patch from a different country on the arm. The soldier held a hand out to me, but I didn't accept his help.

"Are you all right, boy?"

"I am all right," I replied in English.

The soldier glanced at the retreating British soldier, who joined the others in the open field of the Maidan. "Sometimes, they forget who they were and where they came from before they landed here. Brought all their prejudices with them."

He turned back to me. "Are you lost?"

"No." My tears were gone now, replaced by a faint feeling of hope. "I need help. I'm looking for my father. He is a soldier, too. I know he is in Burma, and I must see him."

The soldier pulled a pack of cigarettes out of his pocket and lit a match with the tip of his nail. He took his time inhaling the smoke, savoring the tobacco fumes cascading into his lungs.

I held my breath and exhaled when the soldier did.

"Do you know what his regiment is? I may be able to locate him."

"I—I don't know."

The soldier laughed. "Boy, how am I supposed to help you if you don't know?" After the smoke cleared, the soldier looked at his watch. "Will you meet me here in a few hours, say at five, and give me more information? I'll try to find him for you."

"And you'll take me to him?"

"I'm not sure that's possible unless he's stationed here." A few raucous jeers aimed at the soldier rang out. He grinned in their direction, then turned his attention back to me. "Tonight, bring me more information about your father." The soldier waved goodbye before jogging off to join the others on the Maidan.

I raced back to the house and burst through the door. "Ammi! Ammi!" Echoes carried my voice back to me. I ran into the sitting room and stopped in my tracks. Muhammad was sitting on the couch, holding a trembling cup of chai.

"Haroon." He stood abruptly, almost spilling tea on his white pants. He set the cup down and held out his arms.

"What are you doing here?"

"I'm here to take you home."

I took a step back. "No. No, we can't go yet. I'm so close to finding Papa. I just need a few more hours."

"Chotu, we can't find him," Muhammad held a hand out to me, but I didn't budge.

"You can't, but I will," I said and made to flee the room, but Muhammad caught me and held me back. I struggled in his arms. "Let go of me," I cried, but Muhammad only held on tighter.

"He's gone."

I fell still. "Where's he gone?"

"He's dead. Papa is dead." Muhammad began to sob.

I lay still in Muhammad's arms. To think I'd been running around town to get to Papa when he'd gone and died before I had a chance to reach him.

Ammi stood in the doorway, her eyes swollen, and watched me struggle out of Muhammad's arms. She held out a letter. "It's true, my son."

I didn't move to take it from her. "You're lying," I said to the room. "You're both liars." No one attempted to stop me as I ran back up to my room and threw myself onto my bed.

Papa was deep in the ground now, far away from me, forever out of reach. I curled up and hugged my knees, and howled in pain. I beat the bed with my fists, and then when I had poured out all my tears, I shut my eyes and wished for Papa to return and wake me up from this nightmare.

When I awoke the following day, I felt a deep sense of shame. Papa's letter lay on the pillow beside me, fluttering in the breeze. I reached out and touched the stiff paper. Then, breathing hard, I read his last words.

"Beta," it began, "I'm afraid this is the last you'll hear from me." I put the letter down and waited for the rising tide of grief to subside. "I'm disappointed I only lasted this long. I must hurry and tell you that I love you and that I always will." His handwriting changed to a scrawl, almost like it was someone else's writing, rife with misspellings. "I have to tell you that I've seen the enemy, and it is puzzling. In the jungle, we met the Japanese, and I'm very sure that's whose bullets pierced me. But we met our own. It was like looking into a mirror. Our men suddenly on the other side. It confuses me. I'm confused, and I will die confused. I know I don't make sense; my mind speaks to me in pieces. But, beta, understand that the enemy sometimes isn't who we think it is. It isn't the Japanese or the British or whoever may be the named enemy at the time. Sometimes, it's like looking into a mirror. I know this doesn't make any sense, but I hope someday it will. Take care of yourself and your country. May Allah have mercy on my soul, and may Allah have mercy on India."

I held the letter to my heart, keeping it close for a few beats. There was a part of me that knew, even in my desperation to find him, that Papa had left the earth a while ago. That the last time I saw him would be the last memory I'd ever have of him. That my race to find Papa was only a race against his impending death.

I crawled out of bed and toward the window, leaning my forehead against the bars. It wasn't a dream or a nightmare anymore.

Papa was truly gone.

Before I could close the window shutters, I heard a shout outside. I squinted through the bars and saw a large group of scrawny villagers shuffling down the road. These people reminded me of the model skeleton I'd seen in Dr. Bannerji's classroom: skin painted on, their eye sockets hollow, lips shriveled and cracked like the desert. Their voices were hoarse, and, like a drone of bees, they descended on the town. "Paiter jala," they repeated over and over. I recognized the words. Their stomachs were burning from hunger, they said.

I gasped when I recognized Shah Jehan and her family, their clothes in tatters, stumbling down the road toward Naani's house. At that moment, I felt Papa had brought something back to me. Tears forgotten, I ran downstairs, past my surprised ammi, who lay in a stupor on a couch in the sitting room, and threw open the door. As I hurried toward her, Shah Jehan tripped and fell to her knees, but I caught her in my arms just before she fell to the ground. Then I did something I'd never thought I'd do. I kissed her soft forehead and then the tip of her nose. Her eyes were shut, but she gave me a weak smile. Abdul Uncle and Fatima Aunty knelt on either side of me to help her up.

"Haroon!" Ammi called out. She ran out onto the road to where I sat, cradling Shah Jehan's head in my lap. She looked around her at the slow-moving parade of refugees gathering by the side of the road.

I looked up at Ammi and Muhammad, who had trailed after her. "They're—they're Naani's servants. They're back." Even in her weakened state, Shah Jehan rolled her eyes at me.

Ammi and Muhammad helped Shah Jehan and her parents into the house and led them to the sitting room, where Ammi seated them on a low couch.

"We have to feed them," Muhammad said, wringing his hands. "Should I bring daal and rice?"

Ammi knelt in front of Shah Jehan and her family as a doctor, alert and introspective. She inspected their nails, looked inside their mouths, and examined their eyes. "They're dehydrated; their bodies can't consume solids right now. We have to start slowly, or else they'll become terribly sick. Get me some water," she said to Muhammad, who hurried away.

I watched Shah Jehan and her parents lay still for a while, then headed to the kitchen, where Muhammad and Ammi were preparing a thin soup of daal.

I came around to Ammi and hugged her. "I miss him, Ammi. I miss Papa," I said, my voice muffled by her dupatta.

Ammi held my face in her hands. I asked her what we would do now that he was gone.

"We will do what Papa always wanted us to do. To help others by being good to our people. And those people in the sitting room need our help." Ammi said. "It's what Papa would have wanted."

My tears soaked Ammi's dupatta. "I just want him to come back. How do we make him come back?"

Ammi shook her head and moved away from me. She went back to the pot of food and stirred as she wiped away her tears with her dupatta.

"You can't." Muhammad put his arm around me. "The only thing we have now is our memories of him."

I stared at the floor and nodded. I noticed Papa's letter folded and clasped in one hand—I must have been holding onto it the whole time.

"Papa is gone," Muhammad said. "But we are still here." He squeezed my shoulder and turned back to rummage through the cupboards that contained our own emptying rations.

I made my way to the spare bedroom, where Ammi had set up two beds. Shah Jehan's parents lay fast asleep on one. On the other, Shah Jehan sat watching her parents with large, worried eyes.

I lowered myself on the floor beside her. "We'll take care of you. We'll take care of you until you're healthy and strong again. We'll be a family because that's what my papa would have wanted."

Shah Jehan's eyes widened with realization. "I'm sorry," she tried to whisper.

"You can't be sorry," I said. "And you shouldn't be."

"You're suffering, too."

"I want you to meet my papa." I unfolded the letter and read it aloud to her. When I'd finished, she placed a weak hand on my cheek.

"Thank you," she mouthed, then shut her eyes and fell asleep.

I sat with her for hours, holding her hand in mine and wishing that Papa were with me at that very moment to meet Shah Jehan for the first time.

# FOURTEEN

# THE PROMISE

There was no churail in sight. Maera's glasses fogged up again, and she took them off to wipe them on Rob's tank top. A tree creaked somewhere up ahead. Maera snapped her glasses back on and held the hammer tight, but it was only the leaves crackling against one another. She followed the trail to the two-headed tree from their first attempt, but this time she headed down the track that veered left.

It looked the same as the other one: similar-looking trees and vines lined the path. The foliage closed in on either side of her, whispering to her as she passed. Maera wiped the sweat from her forehead and halted. Her ears twitched at an unfamiliar sound, but it was just the wind.

The trail began to slope downward. Soon, the canopy above Maera opened up, and she was able to see the sky. "Finally," she said aloud and then staggered back when she spotted a long canyon carved into the ground. "What else have you got in here?" she asked the greenhouse. The sky groaned as dark clouds roiled above her.

Tall grass surrounded the canyon. On the other side, Maera could only see more jungle. She squinted to find a moving form, a creature, a human, but she couldn't find anything.

"Hello!"

She received no response. She followed the trail hugging the canyon until she was immersed in the forest again. Behind her, a twig cracked. Maera spun around. "Who's there?" she called out, holding up the hammer. The grass to her right crunched, and she whipped around, breathing hard, and tried to make out the dark shapes in the trees.

Still nothing. Maera wiped her brow again. The muscles in her legs were twitching, urging her to run back the way she had come. Sweat trickled down between her shoulder blades and puddled in her lower back. She kept walking.

The trail began to incline upward. Maera panted and stomped up to the top. Finally, the trees cleared up ahead, and Maera ran to get out of the eerie jungle.

The path ended at a large mossy pond. It was still and green and quiet. Lily pads dotted the surface, but she didn't hear any frogs. There was no other sign of life but for the flora.

She cupped her hands on either side of her mouth. "Hello? Asad!"

Her voice echoed once, then twice, the grass around the pond rustling in response. Maera skirted the edge of the pond and whacked at the grass whipping her legs. Behind her, the trail disappeared from view, but she didn't care. Maera stared at a spot where the grass had been flattened. Someone had been there, and Maera gritted her teeth, fighting against the hopelessness that rose within her.

She scanned the outer edges of the pond and spotted something she hadn't seen before. A separate trail cut through the grass, leading away from the water. It rose upward, and as Maera followed it with her eyes, a small mountain emerged. The path changed from dirt and gravel to spiky rock, leading up to a stone castle.

"What?" she asked aloud, her voice echoing.

Maera took a few steps toward the castle, but the pond's surface began to ripple beside her. The lily pads trembled and floated aside. Pinpricks of fear itched her palms. The water appeared to wrinkle, and a churail arose from the water, her twisted feet hovering in the air.

"I wouldn't go near that castle if I were you," she said in Urdu.

Maera yelped and threw the hammer at the churail. It flipped in the air and landed with a dull plop in the water several feet away.

The churail bared her fangs. Her eyes were dark red, the same color as her lips. "Silly girl."

Maera ran toward the craggy trail to the castle, but the churail, still hovering over the pond, followed her.

"Listen to me," she spoke in honeyed tones. Her voice was inside Maera's head.

Maera slapped her hands over her ears. "You can't control me." Maera pushed ahead until the churail appeared in front of her, floating above the ground. Maera skidded to a halt, her hands knotted into fists.

"There is a creature that lives in there. Much worse than I."

Maera trained her gaze on the churail. "I don't believe you," she said in her best Urdu. "I know what you are."

"What am I?"

When Maera didn't answer, the churail let out a deep-throated laugh. "You can't even say the word."

Maera slipped the pair of scissors out of her pocket and held it up above her. "Don't come near me."

"Whatever it is you're seeking, you won't find it in there."

Her voice sent shivers down Maera's arms. "You're lying."

The churail watched her with an impassive face. For a moment, Maera's heart sank. Perhaps she'd been mistaken. Maybe Asad had never entered the greenhouse that night, just as Jimmy said. This greenhouse could be this strange world with only one inhabitant: the evil creature in front of her.

The churail floated to the ground. Maera stepped back, but the churail didn't pursue her. Instead, she folded her hands and waited for Maera to speak.

"Am I right?" Maera asked. "Is Asad here?"

The churail nodded. "He's been here a very long time."

"I knew it!" Maera heaved a sigh, the humidity in the greenhouse making her lungs work overtime. "I want to see him."

"I'm afraid that's impossible."

"All of this is impossible. I want my brother back." Maera held the pair of scissors out in front of her. "You've had him long enough."

The churail's expression didn't change. "If you want him back, I need you to do something for me."

"What, like three tasks or something?"

The churail held up a long, bony finger. "Just one task."

"No. I want him back now. I'm not doing your bidding."

"You'll do one task," the churail continued. "If you think it will be easy, then you don't know what you're dealing with."

Maera scowled at her. "What is it then?"

The churail gave Maera a fierce grin. "A sacrifice."

Maera shuddered, her insides flooding with fear, but she didn't break eye contact. "Like a goat or something?"

"You'll know what it is when the time comes," the churail replied. "You must promise me."

"Fine, I promise." Maera backed away toward the forest.

She kept a steady eye on the churail till she reached the trees, but when she blinked, the creature was gone. The castle, too, disappeared from the horizon. All that was left was the pond and the still grass behind her.

# FIFTEEN

# THE TASK

The sky was ribboned in blood-reds and oranges when Maera stepped out of the greenhouse. The others were spread across the grass in various poses of sleep. But something about her backyard made Maera reel. She took her glasses off and rubbed her eyes, but when she put them back on, it was still there: the trees along the outer edge of her backyard had grown denser. Maera wasn't entirely sure, but she thought she saw a few vines dangling from them. She shook her head and slipped into her sleeping bag. The rustling made Jimmy twitch beside her; he opened his eyes and squinted at the light.

"It's early," Maera said. "Go back to sleep."

"You're still wearing your glasses." Jimmy sat up suddenly and pulled his arms out of the sleeping bag. "I knew you'd try and go inside without us. The churail is dangerous."

Maera glanced at Sara and Rob, then lowered her voice. "I talked to her."

"You did what?"

"Shh!"

Jimmy's eyes were large and horrified. "She could have hurt you."

"She couldn't. You said it yourself. She seeks revenge against men. She didn't try to attack me or anything. Only talked to me."

Jimmy rubbed his jaw. "You must have been in there for hours."

"It only felt like one hour. Or maybe less. The trail took me out of the forest and to a weird pond. There was a creepy-looking castle, too."

"Wow." Jimmy studied the greenhouse, its light fading as the sky brightened above. "There is a whole world in there."

"But no life. I went in looking for Asad, but all I saw was the churail. She told me not to go inside the castle."

"Why?" Jimmy pulled the diary out of the sleeping bag and hugged it to his stomach.

Maera scoffed. "She said I wouldn't find what I'm looking for in there. Asad could have been in there, locked away all these years."

She looked back at the house. Did her mother know that, while she slept, Asad was trapped somewhere in their own backyard? That he was so close to them after so many years apart?

"And she tried to negotiate with me," Maera said.

Jimmy surprised Maera with a smirk. "Demons are the best hagglers."

"She wants me to complete a task for her to get Asad back, which I promised to do. I just—" Maera looked away and chewed the inside of her mouth. "I think I'd rather circumvent all of that and break into the castle. He's there. I know he is."

"Maybe you should do what she asks," Jimmy said. "No good ever came from breaking your word."

Maera took her glasses off and rubbed her eyes, weary after a night without sleep. "I don't feel like I owe that demon anything."

"You already made a pact. I wouldn't try to break it."

Maera glanced at Rob's and Sara's sleeping forms again. "Don't tell them about this. It's best we keep it to ourselves."

Jimmy nodded. He held up the diary and turned it over and over in his hands. "Do you think she will try to break out and attack us?"

"I don't get that feeling. And that's all I'm working on now."

"Maybe this will help," Jimmy said. "I found these last night. Our naana held onto these small scraps of papers and tickets and hid them in the pages. Like this diary is a box of memories he wanted to revisit. One scrap was that letter to Shah Jehan. The others are here." Jimmy opened the diary and held up a folded piece of paper along with what looked like a clipping from a newspaper.

Maera took the folded piece of paper, sure its contents were more interesting than mere scraps and a newspaper clipping, and opened it quickly. "It's old." The page was covered with scrawled, hurried writing. She handed it to Jimmy. "It's written in Urdu."

Jimmy held the letter gently in his hands as he scanned the page. "It's . . . this is very sad. This is a letter to our naana from his father before he died. Our naana followed his father to the war front and never got to see him before he died."

Maera compared the letter with the few memories she had left of their naana.

"Wow," she said. "This is what your mom meant by the war devastating him."

"It could be." Jimmy looked away, his eyes bloodshot.

"I'm sorry."

Jimmy sat back against the sleeping bag. "I got to see my father before he passed. We spent a lot of time together. We knew he was sick for years. It wasn't like this, leaving his son to learn about his death through a letter. This—" Jimmy held up the letter. "This could help explain who our naana was."

"I don't want to know who he was," Maera said.

Jimmy held the diary tighter and said in a small voice, "We should still read it."

"As long as it helps us figure out why these things are happening to us right now."

Maera stared up at the sky as the world around them awoke. Birds chirped in trees, cicadas began their droning, and the sun rose bright and hot above their heads. But even as the new day began, she couldn't shake herself out of The Past.

"It almost makes me feel bad for him. Almost makes me wish I knew him better."

"Me too," Jimmy said. He folded the note and opened the diary at random to place it back between the pages.

"But what is he not telling us?" Maera asked.

Jimmy held up the newspaper clipping, but Maera waved it away. "I could Google whatever that is. It's not going to give me what I want."

Jimmy sighed and flipped the pages back and forth, only to return to the same page. He leaned into the diary and read aloud in Urdu, then translated it for Maera, though she'd understood more than half of it. "This is the only information he has on the churail from when he was in Bengal. The way to prevent one is to treat a woman well."

"That's great advice." Sara yawned and unraveled herself from the blankets. "You men should always be treating us well."

Jimmy smiled to himself and followed the Urdu letters with his finger. "He wrote that a churail was a woman who was treated badly by the men in her life. When she dies, she becomes a churail. And she takes revenge on men."

"If she's trapped in there, she was trying to take revenge on our naana."

"And maybe she failed." Jimmy looked up at Maera. "Our grandfather must be the reason she exists."

Maera felt the resentment coil inside her like a tightly wound spring. She pounded the grass with her fist. "This is so fucked up." Sara winced at the word. "I was sitting here feeling bad for him, and now it looks like he went around creating churailain. And then he dies, and we are still dealing with his mess."

The greenhouse's light had dimmed, but its insides shuddered at Maera's words.

Jimmy reached out to stop Maera from gouging out chunks of grass and hurling it at the greenhouse. "We are his only grandchildren now. I think our naana made this house appear in your backyard and left me his key to his diary so we can fix his mistakes. I don't believe what our mothers said. It's not like he's cursed us."

Maera swatted his hand away. "He did curse us because losing Asad broke our family. It's his fault we lost him. It's his fault Mom and Dad stopped getting along; his fault that Dad walked out on us. When this is over, let's burn that thing."

Maera stared bitter daggers at the diary. Jimmy tightened his grip on the book. "It doesn't say what our naana did to create the churail."

"Yet," Maera said. "We haven't gotten to that part yet. And, I'm sorry, are you defending our grandfather?"

Jimmy was taken aback. "You may feel like he cursed you, but you forgot about my family."

Maera looked away to stare at the ground in front of her.

Jimmy went on. "Cancer isn't a curse; it's biology. When my dad left us, he was in a state of bliss. He was ready to let go of everything. His death didn't force my mother and me apart."

"Then the burden falls on my family. He cursed only us. And you and your mom get to live happily ever after."

Maera eyed Jimmy. He flinched as if he'd been struck in the face. "Happily ever after does not exist. We are moving past our grief, and we are moving on with our lives. It's what my abbu wanted. Maybe it's what our naana wanted too."

Maera stood up and paced in front of the greenhouse door. She turned to Jimmy and held out her hand. "Give me the diary. I'll translate it myself."

Jimmy didn't move.

"I said, hand it over." Maera's hand shook. She was fully aware of how sleep-deprived and cranky she sounded.

"Guys, please," Sara said, sniffing away tears. "Please don't do this. It's turning you against each other. Your naana might have been the villain in the story, but he isn't anymore. He's gone, okay?"

"His presence is right here," Maera said, pointing at the greenhouse.

"He couldn't have been that evil." Jimmy shook his head. His voice was soft as he stared at the ground. "He fell in love with Shah Jehan."

"That doesn't mean anything," Maera retorted, though she felt a twinge of regret. There was a small place where she kept the scant feelings she had for the grandparent she hardly knew.

Sara scooted closer to Jimmy and put a comforting hand on his own. She looked up at Maera with her large, pleading eyes. "Maybe the churail wants to come between you two so that you don't work together to get rid of her. Your naana was counting on you guys."

"He hasn't redeemed himself until I see Asad. Keep that diary for now. But when this is over, I'm going to enjoy watching it burn."

"Sara's right," Rob said. The three of them turned to him. Maera couldn't help noticing that his hair was adorably disheveled as he sat up in his sleeping bag. "You both should work together. In fact, we all should. I know you're upset at the greenhouse or whatever is inside, but we're with you in this." Rob stared hard at Maera. His gaze was so forceful that she had to look away. "You don't have to do this alone. We're with you."

Maera flushed and nodded, a mix of anger and frustration constricting her chest. "You're right. You're all right."

"That's the smartest thing you've said the past two days." Sara smiled at Rob.

Rob grinned back at her. "That's the nicest you've been to me the last two days."

Maera took off for the house before anyone could stop her. It was still dark inside; the morning sunlight hadn't made its way into the house yet. She slipped through the shadows to face Ammi's bedroom door. She held up a hand to knock but stopped herself from waking Ammi.

The door hinges creaked as she pushed it open. Maera winced, waiting for her mother to awaken, but she lay still in her bed. Aisha Khala was on the other side, facing away.

Maera tiptoed in and headed for the bathroom, where she knew Ammi kept her hairbrush perched on the edge of the sink. She picked through the bristles and pulled out a clump of hair, dark strands interspersed with too many grays, then bundled them up in her hands. She recalled years ago when a more superstitious Ammi had made her mock-spit on her hair before throwing it away. She said spitting on it kept evil spirits from taking her hair and doing nefarious things with it. This must be what the evil churail wanted as a sacrifice.

As Maera stepped out of the bathroom, Ammi stirred and opened her eyes. She squinted in the dark. "You're up early."

Maera froze. "I came in to check on you after last night's call with your cousins."

Ammi lay back against her pillow. "We're all right. We always are. We Khan women are made of strong stuff." Maera kept her hand balled up around the hair as she sat on the edge of Ammi's bed.

In the dark, Ammi smiled at her and took Maera's free hand. "Let's get more sleep," she said. "I need sleep. Maybe everything will go back to normal once we all get some sleep."

Maera squeezed her mother's hand. "I'd love that," she said. "But maybe if we could get a waking minute just for the two of us, we could talk about some things?"

Ammi's eyes closed, and her breathing became deeper. Maera sighed and waited until her mother was asleep again to creep out of the room. She rummaged for a ziplock bag in the kitchen, stuffed Ammi's hair into it, then rolled it up and stuffed it into her pocket. The touch of hair still tickled her palms, and she rubbed her hands together to brush the phantom strands away.

Maera glanced through the kitchen window at Sara and Jimmy sitting close together, heads bent toward each other, while Rob rolled up his sleeping bag behind them. He said something to Sara and Jimmy and waved at them.

Maera hurried to the patio door and slid it open. The morning had already grown hotter; sweat had stained her brow in seconds. Across the backyard, Rob turned his back to her house.

"Hang on," Maera called out. Sara and Jimmy scooted away from each other, busying themselves up with rolling up sleeping bags and folding blankets.

Maera caught up with Rob. "You're leaving already?"

"I need to brush my teeth."

"I don't think your breath smells bad. I mean, not that I'm close to your mouth anyways."

She pressed her lips together and looked away, wondering where that thought came from and what exactly made her so horribly awkward around Rob.

"Why don't you stay for breakfast? I make pretty good scrambled eggs. Super fluffy."

Rob looked beyond her to Sara, who walked over with his blankets. He took them with a grin.

"It's true," Sara confirmed. "She makes really good eggs. Why don't you stay?"

"I'll put these things away first." Maera watched him go, avoiding the heated stare she was getting from Sara.

"I'll be your sous chef," Sara said with an encouraging grin.

"Can you get a bowl and five eggs ready for me, sous chef?"

Sara didn't move. She crossed her arms and pouted.

"Please?"

"That's the Maera I know." Sara jumped up and hugged her. "You don't have to be alone. Don't forget about the rest of us, okay?"

Sara let her go and headed for the patio door. Maera approached Jimmy standing next to the greenhouse, peering through the door.

"Hey." Maera nudged Jimmy with her elbow. "I got the task done."

She pulled the ziplock bag from her pocket and met his grimace with her own. "I know." When she touched the handle, she felt it tick under her hand like a clock. She swung the door open and hurled the plastic bag inside.

"Happy?" she called. The peepal trees shook at the sound of her voice.

Maera slammed the door and peeked at the dirt trail in front of her. The plastic bag had disappeared.

"That's her task done," Maera said. "Now we wait."

# SIXTEEN

# THE WEDDING

Cawnpore, India, 1947

The evening I followed Muhammad and Shah Jehan to my best friend Vikram's house, the sun was setting, and the air was warm and dry. Shah Jehan's bright bangles, borrowed from Ammi, glinted off the street lamps. She caught me staring again, even though I lagged several feet behind them.

She spun around and struck a filmi pose. "Don't I look just like Suraiya?"

I beheld her against the setting sun, and I was speechless. The sequins on her sharara twinkled gold and orange, and her beguiling eyes lined with kohl danced as her soft hands covered in mehendi gestured me closer.

I felt my breath catch in my chest. "You look just like her."

"Oh," Shah Jehan sounded disappointed. "Oh, all right."

Muhammad stared at the two of us. "You might look like Suraiya, but you're a better actress than she is."

"Hai!" Shah Jehan slipped off her shoe and made to thump Muhammad over the head. He giggled and ran to hide around the corner.

"I'll get you back," she said to Muhammad. "And you," she turned her dark eyes back to me, "hurry up, or we'll miss the baraat. And don't be so gloomy."

I jogged up to her, my stiffly ironed clothes rustling, and glowered at the long road ahead.

"You're hopeless," Shah Jehan joked. "Hopeless."

I crossed my arms, feeling like a little boy again. "I hate weddings. What's the point of all these ceremonies? Just say you want to be together, and that's it."

"What about when I get married?" Shah Jehan asked. "Or when you do? Will you be this miserable?"

I grumbled under my breath and walked faster.

"Speak up," Shah Jehan commanded, the ends of her dupatta fluttering as her dainty feet caught up with me.

"It's too soon to be thinking about things like that."

Shah Jehan chuckled. "I think you're rather protective of me. Like a caring . . ."

I hoped she wouldn't say the dreaded word: brother.

". . . friend." She reached out to touch my arm. I felt the warmth from her fingertips for a moment, and then she poked me with a sharp elbow.

We turned the corner to find Muhammad waiting under a streetlight, a smirk on his face. Behind him, Vikram's house was lit up in reds and greens and yellows, and the doorway festooned with long garlands of flowers. The sounds of the dhol and singing streamed out of the house and onto the street. Shah Jehan squealed and ran ahead, her payal jingling with each footfall. I watched her sweep the curtain of flowers aside and wave at her friends. She soon disappeared from view.

Muhammad leaned against the pole, smiling in her direction. "Doesn't she look beautiful?"

"She always does."

"Chotu. You have to speak to her. Tell her."

I was suddenly warm under my collar. "You know her. She'll laugh in my face and change the subject, and I'll feel stupid. What do you know about love, anyways? And yet, you're always giving me advice."

Muhammad's eyes gleamed with mirth. He put his hands up in mock resignation. "Now listen. Just because I've sworn to be a bachelor for life doesn't mean I wouldn't know."

"Let's just get through this shaadi," I said, glaring at the house. "I hate shaadis."

Muhammad grabbed me by the shoulders and shook me. "You're an old man before your time!" He ran toward the house.

I waited, listening to the revelry echoing in the night. Though it was still warm out, I felt a sudden eruption of goosebumps on my arms. A twinge of apprehension inched its way up my spine on a pair of spindly feet. The last time I'd felt that way was years ago in Bengal, the day I saw things that didn't seem believable later. As the night continued to deepen, a bird cried out with a screech I still remembered in my dreams. Kallikakundu.

I hastened to get out of the semi-darkness and into the bright glow of Vikram's courtyard. Strings of lights and flower garlands snaked around railings and fences, and candles covered every available surface. A group of girls pushed past me; I followed their tinkling laughter to the sitting room, where I found Vikram's sister with her friends, blushing and looking demure. She was covered head-to-toe in red and gold. Jewelry glinted from her forehead, throat, ears, and nose; bangles weighed her arms down. It was as if she were made of light.

She caught my eye and waved at me. I waved back, then felt an arm around my shoulder.

Vikram sidled up to me and peeked into the room. "Look how happy she is. If I could live another thousand years, it would be to see that happiness on her face every day."

I threw an arm around my strapping friend. He was impossibly chiseled, blessed with a strong jaw, his thick, wavy hair tamed with gel. I tried not to be bitter, but he was just the kind of man Shah Jehan liked.

"We'll miss her," I said. "We are giving away one of our own."

Vikram beamed at me. "Where are the rest?"

I nodded down the hall. "There's Muhammad." We watched him stuff an entire ladoo into his mouth, stolen from a passing tray. Then, as he reached for another, still working on the one he already had in his mouth, we burst out laughing.

Vikram cleared his throat. "And Shah Jehan?"

I felt a tap on my shoulder.

"Right here." Shah Jehan smiled at us as we turned. "Namaste." She placed her palms together.

Vikram cupped his hand and, trembling, brought it up to his forehead. "Salaam."

"Wah, Babuji," she teased. "You're looking well."

"You—you look . . ." Vikram stood dumbfounded, mouth hanging open.

175

Shah Jehan put up a hand to stop him. "I know; you don't have to say it." She squeezed between us to leave the room.

"Uff, you're just feeding her ego," I said, and Shah Jehan glanced back at me, eyes twinkling. She slipped next to the bride and whispered something in her ear. The girl gave her a tender look, then hugged her.

As I stared at them, Vikram pulled me aside.

"Oh!" I blushed. "I forgot where I was for a moment."

Vikram sighed. "Me too. Come on." He led me past the other guests to the back of the house. We wove through children chasing each other and ducked into the garden to where they had erected a mandap. Under a canopy supported by four pillars, someone had arranged four cushions decked out in red and gold. A pandit knelt on the ground, tending to the ceremonial fire. It crackled and rose higher.

"You both did amazing work," Vikram said. "I'll always be grateful for your help. We all will." He gave me a meaningful look. "No matter what happens."

"So, you've heard." I looked down at my feet, suddenly feeling responsible for all the wrongs of the world.

Vikram stood firm by my side; his indestructible confidence put me at ease as always.

"Whatever's happening in Punjab, it doesn't matter who started it. Muslim or Hindu or Sikh. They're murderers, plain and simple. Carving 'Jai Hind' and 'Pakistan Zindabad' onto bodies—I don't care who they are. They aren't human." Vikram choked on the words. He turned his head to the house, where I was sure Vikram could picture his sister, joking with her friends, untouched by the carnage.

I thought of Shah Jehan then, laughing with Vikram's sister, also protected by the peace in Cawnpore. I tried to speak, but a sudden fear that the senseless bloodshed could occur in here sent bile up my throat, where it balled itself into a fist. "They say Pakistan is our country now," I managed. "But we don't want to leave."

"You don't have to go; this is your home," Vikram said. "This is your country. It always will be. No matter your faith." He glanced at his watch with a worried look on his face.

"Trains are sometimes delayed, aren't they?" I said, reading my friend's mind.

"The groom is always late." Vikram laughed. "Even when they came to ask for her hand, they were late."

I felt it again: the fear, the phantom hand gripping my heart. Inside the house, the noise had died down. Then, suddenly, terrified screams shattered the quiet. The pandit stood up and stared at the house as the ceremonial flame behind him flickered and began to diminish.

"Go, my sons," the pandit said, pointing in the direction of the shouting. "Something's happened."

We ran back into the house together. Terror rose in my chest again; I found I'd been holding my breath the past few minutes.

Vikram reached the front door ahead of me. He staggered back when a man appeared in tattered, bloodstained clothes with an open gash on his forehead. I recognized him as Vikram's cousin.

"What happened?" I asked as I approached them.

Muhammad was beside me in a flash, parting a throng of wedding guests crowding behind us.

Vikram's cousin put a shaky hand to his forehead, his eyes widening when he saw the blood on his hands.

Vikram accosted him. "Where are they?" he asked. The guests behind us quieted.

"They were ambushed," the man said. "Attacked."

"By whom?" Muhammad asked, a quiver in his voice.

The man stared at Muhammad and me. "Muslims," he said, then fell into a faint. Vikram's sister began to wail, followed by a rising torrent of screams.

Vikram caught the man as he went down. He looked up at us.

"Leave."

Shah Jehan pushed through to my side, her hand suddenly in mine.

The man in Vikram's arms groaned. "Dead. All of them." He covered his face with bloody hands.

Shah Jehan bit her lip and turned back to the bride, who was briskly carried away by her friends. Her cries receded. The wedding guests grew restless, muttering curses under their breaths.

"We need to leave," Shah Jehan whispered. "Look at the way they glare at us."

I looked back at my friend as Shah Jehan and Muhammad pushed me out of the door, but Vikram didn't see us go. He wept as he held the man in his arms.

The three of us waded through a sea of distrustful faces in the courtyard. Some of the guests clenched their fists, a few hurled insults at us. Shah Jehan wiped her tears as we left the house and turned onto the road.

We struggled to keep up with Muhammad as he picked up speed. "Friends to enemies and enemies to friends," he said to himself.

"I hate when you talk to yourself," Shah Jehan said, tripping on her sharara.

I caught her arm to steady her. We caught up with Muhammad, flanking him as we kept pace with him.

Muhammad led us down a dark street. "When we get home, barricade the doors." He looked around. "Something bad's about to happen tonight."

I bristled. "We were supposed to be safe here. This is our city. It's U.P., not Punjab."

"It doesn't matter." Muhammad took his glasses off to rub the bridge of his nose. "It's human nature. You draw a line in the sand, and people will claim sides. It's already begun."

I balled my hands at my side, feeling helpless again under the weight of the world. "What good is independence then? An arbitrary line is drawn on a map, a line severing us from our friends and neighbors. Some freedom."

"No," Shah Jehan said. Her earrings caught the light from a streetlamp and danced like little flames as she shook her head. "That can't be a reason for murder."

Muhammad watched the street lights wink out, one by one. Then, someone threw a glass bottle against the pavement; its shards scattered on the ground in front of us.

After that, we hurried home without another word.

As we approached the front gate of our house, we could see that every light in every room was turned on. Our family was unaware of the violence gathering around us like a storm. Muhammad waited until Shah Jehan and I were inside the courtyard to slam the large gate shut behind us. Then, he bolted it and backed away.

"What's happened?" Yusuf called out.

Yusuf's wife, my bhabi, trailed behind him, clutching their tiny newborn in her arms. The baby fussed and wiggled, and I gently shushed him.

"Something bad," Muhammad said. "We aren't safe here anymore."

"But the wedding," Ammi said, drawn out of the house as well. "You're missing it."

"There is no wedding." My voice cracked. "They were killed. The groom, his wedding party, Vikram's father."

Ammi gasped, her hand flying to her mouth. "Who could have done such a thing?"

I grimaced. "Muslims. Ambushed them at the train station."

I stared at their stunned faces. "How are you surprised? We did this. We voted them in. They wanted us to have our own country, and that's what they got." I spat the words out. "Britain's marionettes."

Shah Jehan's parents walked into the courtyard, their eyes sleepy. They circled Shah Jehan protectively.

Yusuf looked at me, stunned. "You're saying that we are responsible for this?"

"I don't know!" I glared at all of them. "Who knows who started it? We'll never know because now we're in the middle of another war!"

Outside our gate, a loud chorus of voices suddenly blended into one angry bellow.

"We need to get inside," Ammi said and ushered us back into the house from the courtyard. "Turn off all the lights."

Muhammad shut the door behind us, and we took off, running from room to room, drawing the curtains, turning off lights, and unearthing candles from forgotten places. Ammi led us back to the sitting room. We sat down, our faces illuminated by flickering candlelight.

"Go," Ammi said to Bhabi. "Call your parents."

Bhabi headed for the telephone. We heard her ask for the operator and, with clenched jaws, we waited for relief to soften her voice. If she could speak to her parents and reassure them, there would be a corner of the world where it was still peaceful. Instead, there was only silence. Bhabi stood with the phone to her ear, a horrified look on her face.

Yusuf took the phone from her, craning to listen.

"Hello?" he asked, his eyes wide.

"The lines are jammed." He slammed the phone down. Ammi shrank into her chair.

"The world's gone mad." She turned the radio dial to All India Radio, and a static voice hissed, "The violence in Punjab isn't an isolated incident. Bloodshed is spreading across the country. If you are a Muslim, we urge you to make haste and take only your necessary belongings to the nearest camp. We have a list of missing persons, and we'll begin with—"

"We have to leave," Shah Jehan said, sitting next to me, tears in her eyes. She looked at her parents. "Again."

"We can't just up and leave. This has been our family's home for generations." Muhammad covered his face with his hands.

I looked up at Ammi, who met my gaze with her own. "It was just as Bannerji said. They wanted to split us apart, and they did."

Ammi glanced away first. She probably continued to carry him in her heart, even as I was sure that the complicated man I knew when I was a boy—if he were still in our world—would continue to hold Ammi close.

Outside, the noise grew louder. The mob began chanting, but we couldn't make out the words.

"We have to protect the house," Abdul Uncle said. He gestured to the men in the room. "Grab what you can and barricade the door." He and Yusuf rushed out of the room, dragging the furniture with them. Muhammad remained on the couch, looking deflated.

The sorrow in the room was stifling, pressing in on me from all sides. Bhabi wept, covering her face in her hands, glancing at the telephone at times, but we all knew it wouldn't ring.

I picked up a chair and headed out to help Yusuf and Abdul Uncle. As I piled chairs on top of one another, I was startled by someone banging on the door. The chairs toppled to the ground. The furniture rattled against the door as the banging continued.

I crept closer to the door, turning to place a finger to my lips, while Yusuf and Abdul Uncle looked on. The knocking ceased. We waited, but whoever had crossed the front gate to trespass into our courtyard stayed away.

After that, we dragged our bedding to the front door to take turns guarding the house. Outside, the sounds of chaos continued: gunshots pierced the air, interspersed by ear-splitting screams. Smoke slipped through the locked door, making our eyes water and our noses run. I rolled over to face Muhammad, who had one arm curled under his head, staring up at nothing.

"You were right," I whispered.

Muhammad turned to look at me with his large, melancholic eyes.

"Back when I made you take me to Calcutta," I added. I could make out the grim smile on Muhammad's face in the dark. "And you said you hate history."

"I still do."

"Things will never be the same, will they?" I asked.

Muhammad went back to staring. "Our friends and neighbors, the people we thought were our friends and neighbors, are our enemies now. Whether we want it or not." He shut his eyes and breathed deeply until he had fallen asleep. I lay awake the rest of the night.

In the morning, we dragged our bedding back to our rooms. There was nothing to do but to sit around listening to the sounds of violence. "A full-fledged riot," Ammi said. She hadn't touched her breakfast, now cold. The radio was on, dull voices still listing the names of missing people. Finally, Ammi turned it off, and we were left with the noise of chaos outside.

"I don't know how much longer we can hide out here." I glanced at my big brothers. "We'll die trying to stay here."

Muhammad sighed. "I don't want to leave. There must be some other way."

"We have to go to Moosa. Karachi is in Pakistan now," Yusuf said. "It might be the only choice we have."

Shah Jehan and Fatima Aunty brought in more breakfast, but my family was stonily silent, our hunger replaced by a profound loss of hope.

Someone knocked on the door again. We flinched and exchanged glances until I stood up. "Chotu, don't," Ammi whispered, but I headed for the doorway.

"They know me," I said. "If they haven't tried to hurt us yet, they won't try it now."

I approached the door with Yusuf at a protective distance behind me, holding a pistol low to the ground. As I moved furniture away from the door, Shah Jehan was beside me, helping pull the chairs aside. "You can't be here," I protested, but one look from Shah Jehan made me hold my tongue.

I slid the bolt and opened the door a crack. Behind me, Shah Jehan held my shoulder, her tender hand a source of comfort as I peeked out. There was no one there. I could only see the scars of violence etched across my once-peaceful neighborhood. Three houses were on fire, smoke billowing into the sky. I heard shouts from across the street: boys I knew and had played hopscotch with when I was little were dragging away things they looted. The road was marked with blood and broken glass.

A group of men ran past our house with lit torches. I almost shut the door in fear, but I paused when a pair of eyes suddenly appeared at the crack. It was Vikram with an ashen, angry face, his hair disheveled, knuckles stained with dried blood. He had a rifle strapped to his chest.

He grimaced at me. "Where is she?"

Shah Jehan's grip on my shoulder tightened.

"Whatever you want from this household, you can't have it," I said.

"Where is she?" Vikram asked again.

"Somewhere safe."

Vikram's once lively, handsome face was slack and unflinching now. "Your people took so much from us. My father's body was unrecognizable." His eyes were bloodshot. He glanced behind him at the carnage. "It's only fair that we take from your people what you took from us."

"If that is your definition of fair."

Vikram stared at me, unaware of the turbulent tears streaming down his face. "We're lighting up the houses on this street. We're burning them down one by one. I suggest you take your belongings and get out of here." He looked behind him again. "You have until sunset."

I held onto the door and almost reached out to grab my old friend. "If there is still trust in your heart—"

"Go to your precious Pakistan. I never want to see you again."

I began to shut the door, but Vikram slipped his hand through. "Wait. Wait. Tell her . . . tell Shah Jehan . . ." His voice faltered, and he muttered something under his breath. He turned back to the street and was soon engulfed by smoke.

I shut the door and bolted it while Shah Jehan glared at the ground. "I thought he was going to protect us. To help save us."

"He did."

Shah Jehan let out a cry and fell into my arms like she did so many years ago in Calcutta. I wasn't prepared for such sudden close contact with her, and my heart beat wildly as I wrapped my arms around her. I was certain she'd feel it bursting against my chest as I let her weep on my shoulder. I spotted Ammi and Fatima Aunty standing nearby, and it pained me to let her go.

"Vikram warned us to leave tonight, or they'll burn down our house while we're still inside," I said.

Ammi shook her head. I knew from the way her eyes flickered that memories of our childhood flashed through her mind; our brotherly bond seemed unbreakable at the time. She'd watch us through the window playing gilli-danda for hours. She composed herself and took hold of Shah Jehan and Fatima Aunty. "Get your things together." Without another word, they hurried off to their respective rooms.

Back in my room, I was packing a cloth bundle with clothing when I was interrupted by a transformed Shah Jehan. She wore a black shalwar kameez, and her dark braid was gone, replaced with a short, shaggy haircut.

"I need your clothes," she said.

If the situation weren't so dire, I would have laughed, maybe even teased her for it.

"What do you need them for?"

"They're going to disguise me to look like a boy. So that—" Shah Jehan's eyes flew open, realizing the horror of being female during wartime. "—What's happening out there to those girls doesn't happen to me."

"I—I won't let anything happen to you," I said, small and impotent as I was, cowering in my room while the rest of the world bled to death.

Shah Jehan held out her hand. "For now, give me your clothes."

I found a pair of brown shalwar kameez and handed them to her. She folded them on my bed, then picked them up in her arms.

"They'll be too big on you," I said, but she shrugged.

"That might be better for me."

Hours later, when we met in the courtyard, Shah Jehan was disguised as a boy wearing my shalwar kameez. Yusuf carried a large trunk in which he and Bhabi, who had the newborn snuggling against the cloth strapped to her chest, had placed their belongings. Ammi held onto a burlap sack filled with a meager supply of rice, flour, salt, and spices she'd packed in silver tins. We'd wrapped the rest of our belongings in gunny bags and rolled up our bedding to make it easier to carry. In just a few hours, we'd packed up our whole lives into such little.

Thin red clouds like rivulets of blood slashed the sky. Muhammad glanced at his watch. "We'll have to fit into Abdul Uncle's wagon. If we travel on foot, we'll be ambushed."

One by one, we filed out of the house until it was only me and Ammi left. Crossing the courtyard, I paused and thought of the last words my father said to me.

"We don't have time to miss this place," Ammi said, watching me from inside the house. "The longer we take to mourn, the longer it'll take to leave."

"Did that help you when Papa left us?"

"It did. Sometimes you have no choice but to move on, especially when you have a family depending on you." She took one last look at our surroundings. "Come, beta. It won't be long now till this place is nothing but a pile of ash." She covered her face with her dupatta and walked to the door.

"'May God have mercy on India,'" I said, echoing Papa's last words, and followed Ammi out of the house.

Under a blanket of smoke, we crept single file to Abdul Uncle's wagon, keeping our backs to the wall. Abdul Uncle patted the horse on the head and checked him for signs of distress while the rest of us crowded around the wagon. The streets were oblivious to our flight; the cacophony wore on, uninterrupted.

We threw the bedding into the back of the wagon. Muhammad and I stood aside and let the women in first.

It had to be Vikram who made sure our house was safe from the rioting and looting. Despite everything that had happened, he had found it in his heart to protect us. I didn't know if I'd ever have an opportunity to thank him.

We pulled ourselves into the back of the wagon as Yusuf and Abdul Uncle climbed into the front. Abdul Uncle coaxed the horse to the end of the street. Thick curtains of smoke obstructed our view, so Abdul Uncle turned the wagon around to take the back road, where no car dared venture. We left our neighborhood under cover of darkness. After a while, we stopped at a hill to look down on the city and watched our house burn.

The newborn whimpered and rubbed its face against Bhabi's chest. "My poor son," she said. "To be born into this world."

The wagon rattled along. But soon, we became aware of the crunching of gravel and the rustle of bodies. We realized we weren't alone. Even my infant nephew glanced around wide-eyed, aware of someone's presence.

Suddenly, scores of people emerged out of the smoke, their belongings perched atop their heads. Behind them, cars crept forward, followed by other wagons, cows, and other livestock.

"They're all leaving," Ammi said. "All of them."

Cawnpore Muslims, muhajirs now, marched on, sporting wet bandages and newly opened wounds, as stunned children clutched their parents' hands. The muhajirs' tears were going to leave behind a river, the way they dropped onto the sand to join the ones that fell before them.

I called out to Abdul Uncle to stop the wagon, then slipped down to help a family of parents and a toddler move into the wagon and take my place.

The man nodded in thanks as he put a protective hand on his wife's shoulder and another on his daughter's head. I walked behind the wagon, spotting Shah Jehan's concerned face at times, peeking out to make sure I was still there.

As night fell, we muhajirs left the roads and entered the fields, keeping the River Jumna to our right. Finally, we stopped and spread ourselves out to build a camp. Ammi was back to being a doctor, gliding through the fields with Muhammad and Shah Jehan at her side, tending to the wounded, and consoling the ones who were beside themselves with grief.

Though the constant fear of ambush kept the muhajirs from collapsing in exhaustion, the level of activity began to slow down as, one by one, we took ourselves to sleep. Yusuf and I pulled open the bedding rolls and laid them on the ground while the women stayed cocooned inside the wagon.

I lay on the dirt and stared up at the night sky. The moon singled me out and shone down on me, the bright moonlight preventing me from falling asleep. I threw an arm over my face, but it was useless. My feet twitched and buzzed as if I hadn't stopped walking.

I crept away from the sleeping bodies to follow the sound of running water. The river flowed as it always did, oblivious of our troubles, and I found its idle sounds comforting. I dipped my feet in the cool water at the river's edge and stared up at a sky of stars, wondering what I'd remember many years from now—losing my best friend, my father's home—the moment when my country turned its back on me.

I covered my face in my hands and wept. In the moonlight, I was exposed, and I felt suddenly ashamed.

"I wish you were here, Papa."

I knelt over the water's edge, staring at my murky reflection. After a while, I scooped the cool water to my face, bathed my forearms, and splashed the back of my neck. I cupped water up to my mouth for a drink, but soft footsteps from behind made me halt. The drops of water found their way between my fingers and fell back into the river.

Shah Jehan came into view, drowning in my too-big clothes, her short hair matted and sticking up at the back. I still found her breathtaking. Her quick eyes shone in the moonlight, taking in my tear-stained face. I turned away and waited for her to settle down next to me. She pulled off her chappals and dipped her feet in the water.

"Three more days of running," I said as the waves lapped against our feet. "Was it like this when you left Kallikakundu?"

Shah Jehan stared at the river. "I try not to think about it," she said. "It was hunger that drove us, that kept us on our feet until I found my way to you."

My face grew hot, and I smiled to myself.

"Your family saved us." Shah Jehan slipped a hand through my side to hug my arm. She laid her head on my shoulder. I dared not move for fear I'd disturb her, and she'd run back to the wagon, leaving me on my own again.

Shah Jehan yawned. "If it wasn't for you, I don't know what would've happened to us."

I rested my head against hers. "You're a survivor. You would have survived. And now, you're my good luck charm to get us to the other side of the border."

Shah Jehan snorted. "For a while, I've felt like wretchedness follows my family around. What does freedom even mean anymore?"

"It means I'm here now with you," I said.

Shah Jehan sat up and stared at me. "We're your servants, and we'll be your servants on the other side. So what exactly is freedom for us?"

I wanted to put my arm around her and hold her again. Instead, I took a fistful of earth and crumbled it in my hand, feeling useless as always. "I shouldn't have said that."

Shah Jehan looked up at the night sky. She watched the stars for a moment, eyes darting as if she were counting them. "We wanted to help your family because you helped us. But, on the other side, if we ever have a home again, I will do something with this life I have. I'm going to college to become a doctor like your ma. I'll be able to help people, and I'd pull my parents out of our cycle of misery."

"You will, King of the World."

Shah Jehan turned back to me, her chin tucked. She smiled through her lashes. I held my breath as she moved her hand to touch my face. Her eyes drifted over my shoulder, and she suddenly stiffened next to me. Shah Jehan crawled back from the water's edge and pulled me up beside her. She tried to speak, but her lips trembled, and she pointed at the river instead.

I squinted to see some bulky objects float by, hurriedly passing us as if on some busy errand. It took me a while to realize what they were: corpses, water-logged and bobbing past. I tried to count, but there were too many slashed and bullet-riddled bodies. The remains of men, women, and children knocked each other while their belongings and dead livestock jostled past. There was no way to tell whether the bodies belonged to Hindus or Muslims or Sikhs from where we stood. It wouldn't have mattered. They were all slaughtered and dumped into the river for the same reason.

The current pushed most of them onward, but three of the bodies shuddered and floated to the edge of the river. They rose out of the water one by one, clad in white saris, long braids rippling in the wind, beads of water dripping off them like gems. As they strode out to the opposite shore, we could see that their feet were twisted backward.

Shah Jehan recoiled. I clutched her to my chest, both unable to look away. Two of them disappeared into the brush, but the third one stopped, cocking her head to one side. She turned around and spotted us across the river. We stared back, trembling against each other. Between us and the churail, the river picked up speed, hurtling the bodies to wherever it decided was their final resting place. The churail eyed us and then parted her blood-red lips to say something.

Shah Jehan pulled away from me to run, but I held her hand to stop her. We glanced back across the water, but the churail was gone.

"Tell me you saw it, too," I said. "Tell me I'm not dreaming."

"I saw them," Shah Jehan said. "I never forgot."

Memories broke through to the surface. "All these years, I refused to believe what I saw back then. I thought it was a nightmare."

"It's this violence that's creating them," Shah Jehan said. "Imagine what horrible things those women endured to become churailain."

I let go of Shah Jehan's hand. "Are you pitying them? Don't you remember what they do to men?"

"Maybe they deserve it. Men create wars. The world I've seen now is far more terrible than any churail. The only truly fearsome creatures I've seen are the ones I thought were my friends." Shah Jehan turned her back to me. "We can't go to Delhi. We have to tell the rest," she said. "The river flows down from there."

"This massacre might not have happened in Delhi." The rush of water behind me was no longer calming, now forever sullied, almost nauseating to hear. "We don't have a choice, Shah Jehan. We have to try to get to Delhi. We have to try. We don't have anywhere else to go."

Shah Jehan gave me a look over her shoulder and stormed back to the camp. Behind me, the river quieted, the last of the corpses out of sight. I followed Shah Jehan back through the field and watched as she climbed into the back of the wagon and snuggled close to her mother.

Sitting next to my sleeping brothers, I listened to the wagon creak from Shah Jehan's tossing and turning. I thought of the churailain I'd seen, how they made my blood turn to ice, how baffled I was by Shah Jehan's empathy for them.

On the third day of our flight from Cawnpore, our caravan was met by a rainstorm. The rain fell in thick gray sheets around us, turning the path into a slurry of water and mud. Abdul Uncle's wagon shuddered, the horse whinnied and pulled with all its strength, but the wagon refused to move any further.

With the rain beating down on our heads, we unloaded our belongings and continued the journey on foot, unhitched horses and cows trudging along, their hooves squishing in the wet mud.

Shah Jehan walked alongside. "I hope there's sunshine on the other side. And dry clothes." It was the first time she'd spoken to me since we'd seen the churailain. More than once, Shah Jehan attempted to take my hand.

"What if someone sees you?" I asked, lowering my voice so our families couldn't hear.

Shah Jehan kept her head down, careful of her footing. "I'm just a nervous little brother who needs comforting. I wanted to tell you . . ." she hesitated. "You were right. It's not easy for me to admit that you were right, so don't go around celebrating."

I smiled and squeezed her hand. The rain poured down our elbows and found its way between our hands. Eventually, we were forced to let go.

The following morning, our caravan reached the gates of Purana Qila, a relic from a bygone era. We were delirious from exhaustion. My tongue was dry and stuck to the roof of my mouth, my legs still damp from a mixture of rain and sweat. The world swayed from side to side.

I staggered up to Shah Jehan and pointed at the fort, forcing my tongue to speak. "This is where you're supposed to reign, Shah Jehan. The center of the world."

Shah Jehan licked her dry, cracked lips. "I hope they have fresh water at the center of the world."

The caravan made its way up the busy, dusty road, swarming with refugees, their carts and cars jostling for space as we made our way into the fort. Once inside, I stopped, aghast at my surroundings. What was once a majestic hub of the Mughal Empire, a breathtaking garden at the center of the world, was now packed with shabby white tents, listless people shuffling among them. Guards belonging to the Muslim League stood by to guide the newcomers. Muhammad and I approached them; a cautious Shah Jehan followed close behind.

The guard took the horse's reins from Muhammad's hands without so much as a greeting and led him away.

"That's our horse," Shah Jehan said, reaching out to pet its muzzle, but another guard stood in her way.

"You'll get it back."

Another guard whistled and waved his hands at us, and we followed him to a row of tents. Only one was available to house all of us.

"How can we all fit in here, bhaisaab?" Abdul Uncle asked.

The guard mopped his forehead. "It's all we can do for you at the moment. In the meantime, I can help you get some water." He handed a pail to Abdul Uncle.

"I'll fetch water. The rest of you get settled."

"We'll go with you," Yusuf said as Muhammad took the pail from Abdul Uncle's hands. The three of them headed for the communal well to join a queue of over a hundred people baking under the sun.

Shah Jehan and I each rolled out a set of still-damp bedding, covering clumps of springy grass on the ground. Bhabi and the baby took one bed with Shah Jehan. The baby wriggled, fussy from being too hot. Bhabi sang to him in a quiet voice until he fell into a fitful sleep.

From the other end of the tent, Ammi watched them for a while, then turned her tender gaze to look at me. "I remember when you were that small."

I put my face in my hands. "Ammi, no." I snuck a glance at Shah Jehan, who smiled at my mother.

"Ammi! You used to call me Ammi," she said. My mother moved to lay down next to me. Her breath tickled the side of my face. With her so close to me, I suddenly felt like a vulnerable little boy again.

"Do you think about Papa?"

Ammi closed her eyes and smiled. "All the time. There is so much of him in you." She turned her head to study my profile. "Except you let your anger lead you. Your papa never did. He let his mind lead him."

"I'll try to be more like Papa."

Ammi laughed. "Be yourself. Let your papa's legacy be your guide." She stared up at the roof. "I never had a chance to grieve for your father fully. As soon as I lost him, I gained a new family." She glanced over at Shah Jehan, who crawled over to the entrance to look out at the goings-on in the camp. "She's a good girl."

"Too good for this world," I said, staring at Shah Jehan. "Just like Papa. Sometimes I wonder if he were still alive, would we be here in this tent with no home to call our own? If Papa hadn't died, maybe our country wouldn't have gone to war with itself. That everything would have been right in the world."

I turned to look at Ammi, but she'd fallen asleep with a smile on her face.

It was several hours before the others returned with the water: one pail for the seven of us.

"It was all we could get," Yusuf said, sitting down to catch his breath.

"We'll manage," Shah Jehan reassured him. "We always do."

We took turns cupping our hands into the pail and then lifting our tired hands to our mouths. Water took the place of food, cooling off our insides and restoring a bit of vigor to our weary bodies.

When Ammi, Shah Jehan, and Bhabi went to fetch food from the camp's cooks, I was left with Muhammad and Yusuf bickering with one another while Abdul Uncle napped.

"We're not staying here longer than a day." Yusuf held his son in his arms and looked down tenderly at the newborn. "There are diseases in these kinds of camps."

"We have to wait like the rest," Muhammad said. "Be patient and wait for the lorries. You can try to get there yourself. Go ahead and try. I'll watch from here."

The brothers glared at each other.

"We're not going to get anywhere with you two arguing." I was tired.

"I can't do this to my wife, to my little son. If anything happens to them—" Yusuf squeezed his eyes shut. "How soon are the lorries coming?"

Muhammad shrugged. "They said another day or two."

"They," I said grimly. "We don't even have a home yet, but we have a government."

"We do have a home," Yusuf said. "Moosa's flat. As soon as we get into Karachi, we make our way to him."

Muhammad shook his head. "Moosa's flat won't be able to hold us all. Until we file a claim for an abandoned house, we won't have anywhere to go."

I looked up in surprise. "We just take any house?"

"Those entering Hindustan can do the same," Muhammad said. "So many abandoned homes."

"This is madness," I said, blood rising to my face. "I didn't ask for a new bloody government or a stranger's house."

"Chotu," Yusuf said, "we can never go back. But somewhere, there is a home waiting for us."

"I had a home. Don't call me Chotu, either. I'm too old for that."

Yusuf and Muhammad smirked at each other. My stomach growled, and I rolled over onto my side to sleep through the hunger. As a hot, dusty breeze circulated the tent, I dreamed of Papa and me walking the empty rooms of our Cawnpore house together. Whenever I tried to tell him what had happened, Papa put a solemn finger to his lips and continued haunting the rooms with me in silence.

# SEVENTEEN

# THE SACRIFICE

Maera beat several eggs in a bowl, while behind her, Rob and Sara sat at the kitchen table laughing at a joke. Jimmy leaned against the counter beside Maera and grinned in their direction. The kitchen was bright in the morning light and bursting with the smell of food. In that moment, Maera forgot about the churail trapped in that unearthly structure in her backyard, that her long-lost brother would soon resurface. Instead, she laughed along to Rob and Sara's merrymaking, feeling normal again.

Then Ammi walked into the kitchen, small and sad, clad in mourning white. She staggered back when she saw so many bodies gathered in the kitchen all at once.

"Bobby?" Ammi asked with a hand on her heart as she stared at him.

"He goes by Rob now," Maera corrected her, tossing the eggs around in the pan. They quivered and bounced as they cooked.

"You've gotten so tall. I haven't seen you in years."

Ammi's eyes lit up as Rob stood and approached her. The years dissolved from her face. She gave Rob a hug and rubbed his back. Maera realized with a heavy pit in her stomach that Ammi was finally letting Rob back in so many years later. As Ammi held him out in front of her, Maera knew her mother was staring at what could have been. Asad would be the same age as Rob, perhaps standing in this kitchen next to his childhood friend as they visited home from college. At once, the kitchen lost its artificial sheen as the shadows crowded around her.

Aisha Khala stumbled in after Ammi. "What the hell is this?" she asked, looking around in bewilderment. "It's too early for all this."

Jimmy caught his mother's eye and grinned at her.

"Look at that face," Aisha Khala said, bearing down on Jimmy. "That's my reason to get out of bed every day. That darling little face."

Jimmy flushed and tried to wiggle out of her grasp. "You're always embarrassing me."

Ammi and Aisha Khala had identical smiles on their faces as they withdrew from the kitchen, chattering away. Maera mused that this must have been how things used to be before the mothers escaped their tyrannical father to go out into the world, when life had been less of a burden for both of them.

"That's the happiest I've seen her in a long time," Sara said.

"I wonder why." Rob beamed at Maera, sliding in next to her to make coffee.

They ate in silence. Maera couldn't taste her breakfast—her mind reeled at the thought of fulfilling the churail's task, wondering what it would take for her to see Asad again.

She could hear the mothers walking through the house. Everyone else was free of the burden that weighed heavily on

Maera's shoulders, and Maera found herself glowering at the others around the breakfast table.

Sara lowered her voice and leaned into the table. "When are we going back inside again?"

Looking up from his coffee, Rob spluttered, "I haven't yet recuperated from last night, and you're already talking about the next trip."

Jimmy brushed the crumbs from the table. "I think we should wait."

Sara turned to Maera and touched her forearm, her eyes large and pleading as she shook Maera to get her attention. "We need to find Asad."

"We do," Maera said. "But that greenhouse isn't going anywhere."

Sara looked at Maera and Jimmy. "Last night, we had to go in like our lives depended on it. Like Asad's life depends on it. And now, suddenly, we're backing off."

Maera looked down at the table so that she didn't have to meet Sara's gaze. "I went in alone," she said, her voice rising as she tried to steamroll their gasps, ignoring the "hows" and "whys" meant to interrupt her. "The churail told me she has him. She's not about to give him up that easily."

"They don't hurt women," Sara said, tapping her index finger on the tabletop to stress her point. "You and I can go in and get him back right now."

"I wish it were that simple. You didn't get a look at her face. You didn't feel the terror clawing its way up your throat till you couldn't breathe." Maera shook her head. Her hand drifted to her chest to calm the dread buried deep inside. "I know what she wants, but I can't barter for Asad until I have all the pieces first."

"I don't get it," Sara said, glancing at Rob for support. When he didn't respond, she picked at her eggs, now gloomy and petulant.

"Tonight," Jimmy said. Maera glared at him, but he wouldn't acknowledge her. "Same time and everything. But we will not sleep outside." He rubbed the back of his neck. "It made me very uncomfortable. Until then, we continue to observe the greenhouse and see if anything changes."

Sara smiled at him.

After breakfast, Maera walked Rob to the backyard, avoiding the gaze of the greenhouse as it watched them pass.

"I'll see you later?" Rob asked.

"I guess you will," she said. "Bring more tools too. They came in handy."

At the fence, Rob turned to face Maera. "It's going to be hard to concentrate on anything else today."

He placed an awkward hand on her shoulder. She could feel a pleasant numbness spread from his touch. She waited for him to make another move, but he withdrew his hand and ducked under the loose planks.

When he was on the other side, he waved to her. "See you soon."

Maera chewed on her lip as she watched him go. He kept his head down; his shoulders stooped as he entered the house. She wondered if she'd have the time to figure out the feelings bubbling up inside her, overwhelming her thoughts, before she saw Rob again. She headed back quickly, but a strange sight made her stop. Something had happened to the lone tree in the center of her backyard. Unlike the shapeless trees that lined the outer edge of her backyard, she had this tree's features memorized because her bedroom window looked out on it. It had new growth on its trunk. At some point last night, it had somehow sprouted spade-shaped leaves, the kind that grew on the peepal trees inside the greenhouse.

A thick vine slithered down the trunk and patted Maera on the head. She backed away from the tree and hurried into the house. In the kitchen, Jimmy was alone washing dishes.

"Where's Sara?" Maera asked.

He rattled the plates, startled at her sudden appearance. "She went upstairs to shower."

"Good. I need to show you something."

He turned the water off and took his time drying his hands.

"Okay. Can you move faster than that?"

Jimmy threw the towel aside and followed Maera to the backyard, where she led him to the tree. She pointed at the leaves.

"This is not right." Jimmy squinted at them. "Maybe we carried something out with us. Maybe a seed or a leaf." He looked under his feet.

"It grew overnight, just like the greenhouse appeared one night." Maera pointed to the peripheral trees. They'd grown denser, and several vines swung between the trees.

"I thought my mind was playing tricks with me, but something's happening out here."

"If we brought something out with us, that would mean that the peepal trees from inside grow rapidly," Jimmy said. Maera had her doubts.

"If that's the best you got, then we don't have much time." Maera found a pair of scissors from the haphazard pile of weapons they'd left outside. "She said she wanted . . . something from me. Maybe blood from a relative of Asad's? I'll go in and prick my finger or something."

Jimmy ran after her. "It can't be as simple as that."

"It's spreading. I don't know what that means for the rest of my backyard or my house. I have to go in."

"I'm coming with you."

Maera placed her hand on the door and peered inside. "She knows when I'm coming. She knows when I'm out here holding the handle." And sure enough, the handle clicked in her hand, and Maera swung the door open. This time, she didn't shut it behind her, intent on getting straight to the churail.

Maera ran down the familiar trail with Jimmy following her. At the two-headed tree, Maera took the left path. Jimmy protested, but she held up a hand. "I know the way. The only time she'll appear is if I try to get near that castle."

As they passed the canyon, Jimmy let out a gasp. "So much in such a small place." Maera didn't respond.

At the pond, they surveyed the surrounding fields and fixed their gaze on the castle on the horizon.

"You think Asad is in there?" Jimmy asked.

"He has to be. Otherwise, why wouldn't she let me get close to it?"

They skirted the pond, slapping away tall grass till they reached the craggy trail to the castle beyond.

"Watch."

The pond's surface rippled, and the churail emerged from the green water.

Jimmy raised his fists as the churail floated closer and landed right in front of them.

"Have you brought your sacrifice?" she asked.

"I already gave it to you," Maera said. "The hair from my ammi's head."

The churail shook her head. "A sacrifice."

"What?" Jimmy asked in shock. "You didn't tell me that's what she wanted."

Maera stared at the churail. "We're here now. Take what you need."

The churail drew near, claws extended. Before Jimmy could turn to run, the churail seized him and lifted him in the air. Maera didn't wait to see what happened next. She tossed the scissors and ran for the castle. The grass tugged on her arms and face, slowing her down. Maera pushed through, ignoring the sounds of struggle behind her. The stony path was mere feet away. She flung herself onto the trail. The gravel was loose under her feet, and she slipped and fell, skinning her knees and palms, after which she managed to scramble up the path, half-sprinting, half-climbing to the castle.

The door was in sight. When she reached for it, a blast of

searing hot wind threw her to the ground. Maera fell on her back, only to look up and find the churail floating above her, her hand clasped around Jimmy's throat as he struggled to breathe.

A scream broke the silence.

"What did you do?" Sara's voice was twisted with anguish.

Maera struggled to her feet as Rob and Sara sprinted toward them. Sweat streamed from her pores; her damp clothes weighed her down, tethering her to the ground. The churail chuckled and rose higher.

Sara and Rob finally reached Maera and doubled over, catching their breaths.

"How could you?" Sara had tears streaming down her cheeks. She looked up at Jimmy, who was kicking his legs and trying to pry the churail's hands from his neck.

"I had to," Maera whispered. "For Asad."

"You used him."

Maera was stung by the look Sara gave her; it felt like she'd been kicked in the teeth. She opened her mouth to say something, but she knew there weren't any words to explain why she did what she had to do for Sara to understand.

"She's killing him," Rob shouted and pointed up at the sky. "We need to do something. Now!"

The churail extended her index finger, sharp and thin like a talon, and dragged it across the side of Jimmy's face. A dark line of blood appeared; the churail's tongue snaked out and licked his face. He stopped struggling and screwed his eyes shut. All of a sudden, she dropped him to the ground, where he fell in a heap.

"Jimmy!" Sara threw herself on him. She pulled him up, cradling his body as he struggled to catch his breath. "You're a monster," Sara yelled at Maera.

Maera's gaze caught Jimmy's, and he nodded once in acknowledgment.

The churail showered them with cackles as she landed in between the two pairs. "There is only one monster, my dear, and it is I." She turned to Maera. "Your task. A sacrifice."

"Sacrifice?" Rob stared at Maera. "What is it talking about?"

"I needed to complete one task to get my brother back. She said it had to be a sacrifice, but I didn't get what she meant. It's Jimmy. She wanted Jimmy." Maera looked at the ground; a tear fell from her eye.

From the other side, Sara glared at Maera as Jimmy managed to sit up on his own. He touched his cheek. The blood had disappeared, replaced by a pale pink line.

The churail leered at Maera, her teeth stained with Jimmy's blood.

"Who will you betray next?"

"I—I won't," Maera said. "It was a mistake. This was all a mistake. You weren't ever going to let me have my brother back."

"We can't give up yet." Rob touched Maera's arm. He looked up at the churail. "Take me. I'll be your sacrifice."

Sara managed to get Jimmy to his feet. "Rob, you can't."

"I owe it to him," he said.

Maera's tears fell freely. "No, you don't. None of you do."

She walked up to the churail. "Take me instead. I know your thing is destroying men or whatever, but take me. Take me and let my friends go."

Maera glared at the churail, who stared back at her. As they challenged each other, the ground shifted beneath Maera's feet. The greenhouse began to reorient itself around her.

They were in the middle of the forest again, but there was no trail in sight. Maera was in a small clearing with the churail standing next to her. The sky roiled above; leaves snapped off the trees and swirled around them. The air was heavy and wet: a storm was about to crash down upon her.

Maera faced the churail. "You promised."

The churail sighed and waved to something behind Maera. The grass crunched as someone approached them. Maera turned around and blinked, searching for a familiar form, one she thought she knew so well.

From the forest, Asad emerged.

EIGHTEEN

# THE SEPARATION

Delhi, India, 1947

It had been days, weeks, perhaps—I could no longer tell—until the lorries finally arrived to take us to the train station.

I thought of my house, now likely a pile of smoldering ash and scorched rubble: my bedroom and all my belongings gone forever. My home came to me in a dream once, the bloodshed a distant tremor, and I'd returned to it. I walked around the rooms and touched the floors. But it was useless to dream anymore. The house was gone, and so were the memories we built there. Everything was now buried under a heap of debris.

We packed our belongings in silence. In a matter of days, the tent had turned squalid, and my patience had worn thin sharing the cramped quarters with the rest. Except with Shah Jehan, who shrank further into my clothes, her eyes growing larger, looking like she did when we were reunited in Calcutta. Yet, she never complained. Abdul Uncle fell ill from a sickness that swept through the camp, catching Yusuf unawares as well. When the two could hardly hold down their food and water, she helped clean up their sickness without protest.

Our combined odors weighed the air down in the tent, the lack of a washbasin evident after just one day. Trash piled up in corners. Our clothes were matted and starting to fall apart, clinging to our bodies only through a mixture of grime and sweat. There was constant hunger and thirst, broken by dreamless sleep. The baby cried all night.

How wretched we'd become in such a short time, from living in our majestic house in Cawnpore to end up in this hovel. I would watch Shah Jehan as she sat at the entrance of the tent, as usual, cradling her bundle of belongings in her lap, along with the misfortune that had befallen her family once more. She'd tell me over and over again when she'd see me sulking, "We're together after all."

We carried our meager belongings and filed out of the tent. A crowd began forming a haphazard line facing the gate we'd entered weeks ago, just as the lorries started arriving.

Muhammad, his face now just a pair of hooded eyes and sunken cheeks, caught my stare as we stood outside under the merciless sun.

"We don't know what's out there," I said to him. "Karachi will never be Cawnpore. Wherever we make our home again, I won't pretend everything will be okay."

"Then don't pretend," Muhammad said. "You're allowed to feel this way. But at least get on your feet and do the best you can. We have nothing to do but keep moving forward."

I looked around at the other muhajirs, worse for wear than when they'd first arrived. Some had family members die in the camps, their hopes and dreams for a conflict-free future together hastily buried along with the bodies. Others weren't much luckier. If they hadn't caught the sickness that hit our tent, they'd had limbs amputated from minor sores and cuts that festered into gangrene.

Stories passed from tent to tent of daughters and wives going missing, of women jumping into a well to save their honor. And children, little ones just—it's too hard to write. But ignoring it doesn't mean it didn't happen. What I knew of life when I was a boy, the way I saw things then, shattered into pieces. There was nothing left of our world. We were standing on the edge, about to fall off.

Muhammad pointed at the slow-moving crowd ahead of me. "You think you're alone in all this?"

I didn't reply.

The crowd moved in unison toward that great unknown as one giant wave. It finally made sense then why Shah Jehan kept saying we were all together. It was everyone in the camp, all the muhajirs united in flight. I turned back and found her some distance behind, one arm around each of her parents. She caught my eye and gave me a quick smile.

The lorries lined up outside the fort, and national guards began directing groups of refugees into the back of each vehicle. I was tossed back and forth as I neared the end of the line, and when I turned to make sure Muhammad was still next to me, I found he was no longer there.

"Bhaiya!"

I recalled a distant memory of losing Muhammad in Calcutta, feeling the same razor-sharp jolt I'd felt in my stomach.

I pushed against the tide to reach Shah Jehan and her parents.

"Did you see where Muhammad went?" I asked.

Abdul Uncle swayed on the spot, and Shah Jehan held onto his arm. He shielded his eyes from the sun. "He was with you a moment ago. He may have gotten onto the lorry."

I turned back, but the lorry sputtered and moved ahead. A new one pulled up in its place. "Stay here," I said to them as people behind them shouted and shoved them aside, disrupting the foot traffic. I weaved through the crowd to join the rest of my family.

Bhabi held Yusuf's arm while Ammi nervously scanned the crowd in front of her.

"Over here," I yelled, jumping and waving my arms.

"Where are they?" Ammi asked.

I led them back to where I'd left Shah Jehan and her parents, but they had vanished. Yet another lorry drove onward. "Stay together," I shouted over the din. But the jostling crowd separated me from the others. I was carried with the tide and thrown onto the next lorry.

"Wait," I said, reaching back for my family, but the doors shut just as I spotted them heading to the next vehicle.

The lorry was filled to more than its total capacity. Without a place to sit, I stood against the wall, joining more than half of the refugees in the vehicle. Women cried into their dupattas and sleeves, and children wailed. As my eyes adjusted to the dark, my other senses came alive. It was sour and wretched inside; I could taste the misery in the air. Bile surged up to my mouth. The truck jerked forward, and I stumbled; I shut my eyes and concentrated on the image of a new home.

I held Shah Jehan's hand as we entered it together.

# NINETEEN

# THE MISSING BOY

Asad squinted at Maera. "Who are you?"

Maera froze, not daring to reach out to him as her brother moved closer.

"This isn't right," she finally said. "It's been years."

Asad stopped in front of her. "Maera?" he asked and smiled, a dimple puncturing his cheek. "Is it really you? You look so big." He held up a hand to hover above his head. "So tall."

He was just as she remembered him, just as she'd last seen him, in a blue T-shirt and denim shorts, his wavy hair an unruly mop on his head.

And still only nine years old.

Asad cocked his head to one side. "Am I dreaming?" he asked in his childlike voice.

As he stared at her with an impish smile, Maera's throat constricted, her salty tears burning her eyes. She knelt in front of him and touched his soft cheek.

"You're still so young," she said. "You never got to grow up. You'd be in college now."

Asad's eyes grew wide. "College? Wow!"

He pulled two figurines from his pockets—a cow and a sheep, carved in wood. He lay on his stomach in the grass and made them gallop after one another; most kids played with Legos or action figures, but not Asad. Maera remembered he loved the wooden animals their father had made for him, his one and only boy, something he'd always have to remember him by. Her chest tightened.

A rock rose from the grassy floor, and the churail floated down to sit upon it. She gave Asad a doting look.

"Fix him," Maera commanded. "Change him to the way he's supposed to be."

"This is who he is. Just like he was the day he arrived. Nothing ages in here."

Maera narrowed her eyes. "What do you mean 'arrived'?"

The churail smiled at her. "He arrived outside my door. Just like that."

"We thought he was lost," Maera said. "That he wandered off somewhere."

"My child, no. He was delivered to me. I used to wonder if God truly existed, then He gave me a gift to make up for everything I'd had to endure, after what your naana took from me. A perfect little boy as my gift."

Asad looked up at the churail and grinned. She gave him a maternal smile.

Maera slipped her glasses up to her forehead and rubbed her face hard. "I don't understand any of this. My naana was terrified of you. What could he have taken from you?"

"My child, I knew your naana very well."

The clouds churned above, dipping lower and bringing their wet heat down with them. The churail turned her maternal gaze to rest on Maera. "I am your grandmother, after all."

As soon as the words left the churail's mouth, Maera winced. A familiar feeling fluttered inside her.

"Shah Jehan?" Maera blinked away tears, the realization rendering her numb. "You're Shah Jehan?"

The churail placed a hand to her cheek and smiled. "I haven't heard that name in so long."

"All this time, he has had you trapped in here. All this time. How did you . . ." Maera's voice trailed off; she couldn't finish the thought.

The churail smoothed her sari and clasped her hands on her lap. "If you will be patient and listen, I'll narrate my story."

# SHAH JEHAN

Delhi, India, 1947

I searched for my parents, for Haroon, for his family, but as the last lorry left for the day, I'd realized they had all left. The billowing dust finally settled upon the heads of the remaining refugees. They grumbled and sobbed, then headed back through the gate and back to their grim little tents.

I decided I wasn't going to weep or wring my hands. I was going to find my family. I approached a group of guards, four young men standing in a huddle. They squinted at me as I neared.

"Bhaisaab," I said to the apparent leader, crossing my arms over my chest, feeling exposed without my dupatta, "I need help. My family was pushed into a lorry, and I was separated from them."

The young man had the beginnings of a mustache on his upper lip. He eyed me suspiciously. "What happened to your hair?"

I dropped the pretense I'd worked so hard to maintain during our journey. I was out of danger, no longer in Cawnpore.

"We'd . . . heard stories," I said.

The guard tsk-tsked under his breath and glanced at the trail left by the lorries. "I'd heard some terrible stories, too. I'm glad you're safe, behen. But I'm not sure we can help you. We don't know when the next lorries will arrive."

"My mother has my jewelry. I'll pay you with whatever I have."

The guard rubbed his upper lip and turned back to the others. "Get the jeep," he called to his friends, then turned back to me. "We'll get you to the station right away."

"Shukriya," I said.

The guard smiled at me. He shrugged off his jacket and laid it around my shoulders. I felt comforted by the weight of the coat and closed it tight around me.

"You'll be safe with us," he said.

# TWENTY-ONE

# THE REUNION

Delhi, India, 1947

I ran through the platform searching for a familiar face, my legs quaking as I sped past another recently-arrived group, when I heard a shout. Muhammad was waving at me, separated from the receding crowd. We ran toward one another, and I hugged him hard while Muhammad sobbed on my shoulder.

"We're here," Muhammad said. "Thank God, we're all here." He pulled me inside the station house where Yusuf, Bhabi, Ammi, and Shah Jehan's parents had gathered.

Shah Jehan wasn't there.

"Where is she?" Abdul Uncle asked me. "Where's my daughter?"

I searched their blank faces. She had to be on the last lorry. I left them and ran back out, but the final vehicle had departed without dropping her off.

I went to guard after guard to ask about the next lorry, but they shook their heads and shrugged. Finally, the youngest of the lot put a hand out to stop me. "I can help if you tell me whom you're looking for," he said.

I sputtered out her description. "Her hair is very short, and she was wearing a brown shalwar kameez. She is shorter than me, and . . ." I wanted to describe her striking dark eyes, her beguiling smile, her lips that naturally curved up at either end as if she were perpetually amused by my presence. I'd conjured up hundreds of words to describe what she meant to me and found myself overwhelmed. I reeled, and the guard grabbed my shoulders to shake me.

"I'll send word back. She may be at the camp still," the guard said. "But I will need to contact you if we find her."

I told him I'd wait at the station.

The guard's eyes were kind. "I'll find you." He strode off to speak to the cluster of guards who hadn't been helpful at all. They listened to him and moved to where new lorries had arrived.

Hearing the announcement for the next train to Karachi, I sprinted back inside the station and quickly hugged Shah Jehan's parents. "I'll find her," I told them.

Fatima Aunty cried and clung to me. "Promise me you will."

"I will," I promised. "I'll stay here and wait for her."

Ammi touched my face. "We can't go without you."

"You have to," I said, throwing my arms around her. "I'll be okay. You know I will. Just like I was years ago in Calcutta on my own." I was sure Ammi could recall that time in our lives and know I was old enough to take care of myself.

"Be safe. For all of us," Ammi said, patting me on the cheek. She pulled away and covered her tears with her dupatta.

I hugged Muhammad and Yusuf, while Bhabi brushed away her tears and waved at me as I backed away from them.

"I'll find her. Don't worry."

My family turned and walked to the platform. I waited until they were safely aboard; the train squealed and chugged out of the station. When the steam dissipated, I headed for a row of benches marked "Europeans Only". It didn't matter anymore. The British were long gone now, having distanced themselves from India before Partition tore the country limb from limb. I took a seat and waited, hands clasped in my lap.

There was no sign of her. I continued to wait, the bench's grooves notched into my backside. On the third day of my vigil, as I lay on the bench watching train after train depart, the guard I'd first spoken to ran past me.

I called out to him, and the guard stopped, eyes wild when he spotted me. He helped me to my feet.

"We found her."

My heart hammered in my chest. How horrible I must have looked, standing there in the station, hair unkempt, pathetic wisps of a beard growing out of my chin. And the stink of me! I smiled gratefully at the guard, but the guard looked frantic. My heart pulsed in my throat.

"You better come with me," the guard said and led me out of the station to a small crowd outside. Two men carried a makeshift stretcher toward us, carrying a small person.

"Wait here," the guard said, but I couldn't bear it any longer.

"If she's hurt, I have to help her."

The guard finally turned to face me. "They found her on the side of the road bleeding badly. Someone stabbed her in the stomach." He stopped and took a breath. "They wrapped her up. But she was brutalized. Assaulted."

I couldn't speak. I blinked at the guard, who averted his gaze and trained it instead on the stretcher nearing us. "I don't know if there is much we can do for her, for either of you, except to keep you here and find a doctor who might help her."

The two men stopped in front of me and lowered Shah Jehan to the ground. I held my breath: the combined smell of blood and earth was potent. She was asleep, her hair matted and weighed down with sweat, her clothes stained with dark rust-colored splotches. Her lips trembled—a cut was beginning to scab over on her swollen upper lip.

The guard bent over and studied her ill-fitting clothes. "Who is she to you?"

I picked her up, momentarily shocked at her lightness, and carried her away from the murmuring crowd into the station.

"Bhaisaab," the guard called out, "I don't think there's much you can do for her."

"I'm taking her to Pakistan. I made a promise."

The crowds parted as I carried her across the platform and into the waiting train. I climbed into the compartment and looked for a place to sit, but bulky sacks occupied every seat on the train.

The guard followed me inside. "You'll have to sit on the ground."

"I'll forever be in your debt," I said, lowering my head in solemn gratitude.

"For all the trouble you've been through," he said, nodding at Shah Jehan. "Good luck in Pakistan."

He meant for the words to be comforting, but I felt a cold, steely resentment build up inside of me instead. The guard took my silence for grief and jumped off the train.

I carried Shah Jehan to the end of the compartment and slid to the ground, still holding her close to my chest. Puffs of her breath tickled my collarbone. More muhajirs got on, filling nooks and crannies with their bodies, squeezing themselves between sacks, dampening the walls with the sweat of their fears. I remembered the last time I was on a train—the air crackled with excitement and the anticipation of adventure. There was no such thrill this time.

"We are going to make it," I whispered to Shah Jehan, ignoring looks from the other passengers. I recalled the rumors I'd picked up at the refugee camp of trains arriving in Pakistan filled with nothing but corpses. I held her closer. "Don't worry. We'll all be reunited soon."

She stirred at the sound of my voice. She shuddered and opened her eyes, her pupils large and unfocused, her eyebrows knitted together.

"Haroon?" She reached out, missing my face by inches. She blinked a few times, then placed a hand on her stomach. The magnitude of her injuries became clear to her, and her eyes grew wide, searching my own. I shushed her and rocked her in my arms. Shah Jehan whimpered, tears streaming down from her unblinking eyes.

"We'll be home soon," I whispered. "We'll be home soon."

"I can help you." A man sitting across from us, hugging his knees to his chest, spoke up.

I stared into Shah Jehan's stricken eyes as she blanched. "I don't know what to do for her."

"My name is Ali. I'm a doctor," the man said. "Or I was one."

Ali fished out a packet of tablets from his pockets. "It's all I have. It'll relieve her pain and help her sleep for a while."

I could hardly speak. I took the tranquilizers from the man with tears of gratitude and tipped a tablet into Shah Jehan's mouth. She shut her eyes and swallowed it. Eventually, her breathing evened out.

"There's a clinic in Karachi, just outside of the station," Ali said. "My cousin works there. I feel . . ." The man rubbed his forehead, looked up at the shuttered windows, the decoy sacks sagging in the seats above them. "I feel like saving her would save us. I don't know why."

I didn't understand it either. Putting Shah Jehan together again wouldn't put my country back together. As she rested in my arms, I knew we could never go back, never return to the way things were. Who knew what sort of person she'd become after she healed from her injuries? Who was I becoming as I bore the weight of God's cruelty on my shoulders?

I recalled a line I'd once read, spoken by one of the Mughals. "One of your great ancestors said this, Shah Jehan," I whispered to her. "If you make it through this, if we're together again on the other side—" I choked on the words. "If I could behold the face of my beloved again, I'd give thanks unto God until the day of resurrection." But she continued to sleep, unaware of my little speech.

In Karachi, I hoisted Shah Jehan in my arms and stepped off the train. My legs were stiff from having spent hours cross-legged in the cramped train car. I staggered out and blinked as I looked up at the blue sky, the sky I remembered from Cawnpore, but now it belonged to Pakistan.

As Ali and I made our way out of the station, we were accosted by volunteers handing out water and roti. They tried to pour water into Shah Jehan's mouth, but she continued to sleep, and the water dribbled out of the sides of her mouth.

"We can't do this while she's unconscious," Ali said. "The clinic isn't far from the station. We have to hurry."

I followed him. Shah Jehan twitched in my arms; her eyes fluttered open, and she stared at nothing.

"We're almost there."

The path leading to the clinic was congested with tents and displaced people. Children chased after each other, oblivious to the madness of the world, while their parents sat in a daze. I thought about my family, somewhere in Karachi. I'd find them, but only after Shah Jehan was better again. I shifted her in my arms and followed Ali into the clinic. We headed up a flight of stairs, lined with men of varying ages, some with gashes on their faces and limbs and others wrapped in bandages, making conversation. I slowed down as I climbed the steps, weaving in between patients who looked up at me with curiosity. They moved aside to let us pass.

After bringing us to the women's ward, Ali hurried away while I studied the cramped room. Women in various states of distress occupied every available bed, sometimes two patients in one. Some lay unconscious, their bodies scarred by stitches, clothes caked with blood; their unattended children cried inconsolably next to them.

I turned away from the sight, shards ripping at my throat, when I felt a gentle hand on my shoulder.

Ali appeared with a doctor who was sweating profusely and checking his watch every few minutes. "He'll make sure she gets the best care. Come with us."

I followed them to a small cot set in one corner of the room and gently lay Shah Jehan upon it. The doctor bent over her, checked her pulse, listened to her breathing.

"We gave her a sedative so she could sleep. I think she's in pain," I said.

"What happened to her?"

"She was stabbed. Guards found her by the side of the road. Someone wound a sari around her middle."

The doctor frowned and lifted her kameez. I turned away to let the doctor do his work. Then, after a couple of minutes, I headed to join the men waiting on the stairs. I took a seat half a flight down and rested my head against the wall.

An elderly man nodded at me. "Was that your wife?"

"Yes," I said without thinking. I blushed, imagining Shah Jehan rolling her eyes at me.

"I was younger than you when I married my wife—only twelve years old." The man smiled to himself, his eyes filling with tears. "We have children and grandchildren. What will they do without their grandmother?"

The shared sadness in that building tore at my heart. I kept my eyes shut, pretending I'd fallen asleep so others would keep their sorrow to themselves.

A while later, I'd genuinely dozed off, the exhaustion of the trip creeping up on me, when I was shaken awake by the doctor. I made to get up, but the doctor shook his head.

"This way." He led me down to a courtyard outside. "She has internal injuries. Without proper sutures, she hasn't healed, and her wounds are starting to fester. She has a fever. It could be blood poisoning."

"How long will it take for her to get better?"

"Bhai," the doctor said, "she's dying."

I didn't blink. "You didn't answer my question."

The doctor rubbed his eyes and ran a hand along his bearded chin. He placed his hands together. "I'm sorry. All we can do now is make her comfortable."

"You were supposed to fix her," I said, my voice rising. "I carried her from one country to another, from our home to whatever this place is supposed to be. And you're saying you can't help her? What kind of doctor are you?"

The doctor stared at the ground and crossed his arms.

"There aren't many of us here. And we don't have the capability here to help her. Please, I will do what's best for her."

Then, the tears began to fall. I wiped them away and told the doctor I didn't believe him.

"Miracles don't happen in this kind of place," the doctor said.

I stepped away from him, my tired body shaking, and I crumpled to the ground. I howled in pain, holding my middle so tight that I couldn't breathe. Finally, I lay my forehead on the ground as if I were praying, but there was nothing left to pray for.

The doctor helped me up. "Pay your respects," he said. "I'll pray for you, both of you."

I found my voice then. "I don't need it. I stopped believing in prayers a long time ago."

With my heart breaking into a million tiny shards, piercing my lungs so that I could hardly breathe, I followed the doctor back upstairs into the ward.

"I'm very sorry." He patted me on the shoulder.

I wouldn't look at the doctor, who moved away to tend to another patient. I sat on the edge of Shah Jehan's cot and placed my hand on her cheek. It was clammy and wet; her chest rose in rapid breaths, eyes darting under her lids. I took her hand and squeezed it. Her hand twitched.

"I have to take you home. Wherever that is."

I thought I saw her lips curl into a smile.

There was a sudden commotion behind me. I glanced back at the open door and thought I heard a familiar voice.

Irate nurses descended upon the intruder like winged birds, their white habits flapping. When I glanced above their heads, I saw Muhammad standing in the doorway arguing with them.

"You're here," I shouted, startling the nurses. They quickly moved aside and let me hug Muhammad.

He clapped me on the back. "I knew you'd be here. I checked every day, three times a day even." His worried eyes scanned me. "Are you hurt? Where's Shah Jehan?" Muhammad's face crumpled. "Why are you crying?"

I didn't have the strength to speak. Instead, I led Muhammad to Shah Jehan's cot, ignoring the nurses' protests.

When he saw her, he sank to his knees and gripped Shah Jehan's hand. "This can't be. What happened?"

"The only person who knows is Shah Jehan," I said. "The doctors said we could take her home so she can be comfortable. But do we even have a home to go to?"

Muhammad wiped his tears and looked up at me. "We have a home. I submitted our claim. There is room enough for all of us. The people who lived there, they'd left their food on the table, just like we had. They left all of their belongings behind." Muhammad shuddered.

"I failed them. I failed Fatima Aunty and Abdul Uncle," I cried.

Muhammad continued staring at the ground. "We lost Abdul Uncle."

I pushed back against the wall and found I'd lost the ability to speak. My tongue worked around my mouth, but I couldn't produce any words.

"He had a heart attack on the way over." Muhammad rubbed his forehead. "He couldn't bear losing her."

I remembered Abdul Uncle's cheery face, the rosy apples of his cheeks. He'd become a father to me over the years. I brought my fist down hard against the wall; I'd stumbled into such a cruel world.

Muhammad flinched. "Chotu."

"Don't call me that anymore. I already told you once."

Taken aback, Muhammad's hand flew to his cheek as if he'd been slapped in the face. "Understand that grief is shared around here. You mustn't bottle it up or keep it to yourself. We've lost a great deal, but Fatima Aunty lost the most. This will break her heart. I don't know how much more she can take."

I bent down and picked Shah Jehan up in my arms again; she was alarmingly lighter than she'd been just hours before. "Then I'm taking her to see her ma. I made a promise to Fatima Aunty." I carried her out of the clinic and into the miserable heat outside. Muhammad hurried ahead to hail us a tonga.

The driver took one look at Shah Jehan's pale face and frail body and made haste, speeding in and out of traffic. I laid my head on top of Shah Jehan's, her stiff hair prickling my cheek.

"Almost there."

We pulled up to a large gate. Muhammad leaned forward to pay, but the tonga driver waved away our fare. "Pakistan zindabad," he said. "Good luck."

It made my lip curl hearing it, reminding me of all the sacrifices we made for those two words.

Muhammad led us up to the house and knocked, and almost immediately, Ammi opened the door. She gasped at the sight of us, opening her arms wide to hug Shah Jehan and me together. "You're home," she said, tears trailing down her cheeks. "You're finally home."

I stepped into an open-air courtyard with rooms around the sides. It smelled like a stranger's home, crammed full with another family's memories. The furniture looked nothing like our own in Cawnpore.

I walked through the house, leaving Muhammad and Ammi in the courtyard. The back door swayed in the wind, beckoning me. I ducked to enter an ornate garden with sprawling rose bushes and a small orchard. A covered swing sat in the shade of a few trees, creaking as it swung back and forth.

I looked around at the beautiful garden, cultivated with care by another family. "This is ours now," I said. "You would have loved it. You'd have made it your very own."

I knelt with her in my arms and almost called out to Fatima Aunty when Shah Jehan's eyes fluttered open—she was awake!—and stared at a point above my head, her pupils unfocused. Then, finally, the ends of her mouth twitched, and she smiled.

"Why couldn't it have been me?" I asked, knowing full well what the answer was going to be. "You were always better than me."

Shah Jehan reached up and touched my cheek. "Did I ever tell you—" she began and closed her eyes. It was a while before she opened them again. "Did I ever tell you I love you? Since we first met. I . . . I should have told you."

I touched my forehead to hers, then kissed her lips. She breathed against me and, with what little energy she had left, kissed me back. Then her lips fell slack, and the color left her face.

I felt the presence of others behind me. Yusuf and Bhabi stood in the doorway, along with Moosa and his wife. They looked on with tears in their eyes. Then, Fatima Aunty emerged, dressed in a white shalwar kameez. She was much smaller than I remembered—she seemed to shrink in her clothes as she drew close. Her face was lined with grief.

"She's gone."

Fatima Aunty stumbled forward, and I met her halfway. "No, we have to take her to the hospital," she cried.

"They can't do anything for her. I've brought her back—" The words caught in my throat. "I brought her back so we can say goodbye."

Fatima Aunty let out a cry—a long, sad wail—and hugged Shah Jehan. She gazed at her daughter's face for the last time and placed a soft kiss on Shah Jehan's forehead. After a while, she looked up at me, her face trembling, eyes reddened by tears.

"You'll bury her here," she said and placed a hand on her heart. "So she can always be close to us." She touched Shah Jehan's face. "You were too good for this world," Fatima Aunty said as she stroked her hair and moved damp strands from her forehead. "It didn't deserve you."

Ammi and Fatima Aunty bathed Shah Jehan and wrapped her in a white shroud and lay her down in what would have been her room, on her bed. Then, they retreated to the courtyard with the remaining members of the family to pray for Shah Jehan's soul. But I couldn't pray; I didn't know if I ever would have the faith to do so again. My God was ruthless, devoid of mercy, and if my God had no place in His heart for Shah Jehan or Abdul Uncle or Papa or India even, then I would shun Him forever.

I let the others pray, let them rely on old comforts as I retrieved Shah Jehan from her room and held her close. I asked Fatima Aunty to come out with me, but she shook her head.

"Women aren't allowed at burials," she said, a tinge of disappointment in her voice.

"It's for Shah Jehan," I said, bristling again at the audacity of my God.

"We have to pray instead. It's all I can do for her now."

She glanced at Ammi, who took her hand and soothed her as she lay her head on my mother's shoulder to weep.

I carried Shah Jehan back to the garden where the twins had dug a grave. Muhammad stood aside with his head bowed in grief. He stared at the ground, unable to look at Shah Jehan anymore.

I wrapped the rest of the shroud over Shah Jehan's face with trembling hands, then lowered her body to Moosa, who stood inside her grave. He laid her delicately upon the earth, then reached up for Yusuf to help him climb out. One by one, my brothers took a handful of dirt and let it fall from their fingertips. I did this last, watching the crumbly earth dot her shroud. Yusuf picked up the shovel, but I wrestled it away from him. I wanted to bury her because I knew Abdul Uncle would have wanted me to.

The twins exchanged glances and said a quiet word to Muhammad. My brothers filed out of the garden, leaving me alone in my grief.

I took my time shoveling earth over Shah Jehan's slight form. And with every shovelful, I threw the weight of my anger against the world. My hands were raw and sprouting new blisters; my fingers grew numb from the effort.

It was nightfall by the time I'd shoveled my last bit of earth. I sat beside her grave and put my hand on the fresh mound. Stars were beginning to peek from behind the clouds, and the moon had begun its slow climb.

"Goodnight, Shah Jehan."

The wind picked up, pulling on the leaves and branches of the trees around me. I could hear a rumbling as if a train were hurtling toward me. The earth beneath me trembled, forcing me to my feet. I backed away from Shah Jehan's grave.

From where she lay, a glass-and-wrought-iron structure split open the earth and rose into the air, stretching toward the night sky. Panes of glass and beams of iron shifted and moved in place, while behind me, the rest of my gathered family gasped.

Shah Jehan's anguish had given birth to a greenhouse. It settled itself around her grave.

When the greenhouse finally stopped groaning, we cautiously approached the building. I took the first few steps toward the alien structure and touched the warm glass. It breathed against my hand.

I drew nearer and peered inside: a jungle had cropped up; fronds and vines swayed in the breeze.

Shah Jehan's serene face appeared from within the greenery, her long hair flowing in the wind. She looked at me, a small smile playing on her lips.

By the time the trees stilled, she had disappeared.

# TWENTY-TWO

# THE CHURAIL

The forest fell silent around them.

There were tears on Maera's face. She didn't know when she'd started crying, but she wiped them away. She looked down at Asad as he rested his head on her shoulder. Maera placed an arm around him, pulled him closer. He felt too small, too far away, as he looked up at her with his large eyes, the little dimple imprinted in his cheek.

"So, you created this thing." Maera turned to look at the churail and then at the greenhouse's roof. "He was so protective of this all this time. Of what you created. I can't begin to understand how any of this is possible."

The churail studied her hands, extending her claws until they were the size of daggers. "Perhaps grief is a four-walled thing. Perhaps tragedy has boundaries and shapes."

"And bloodlines," Maera said as Asad pulled away from her and tossed his toys on the ground. He ran to the nearest tree and climbed its trunk, maneuvering around well-known grooves and bumps.

Maera watched her brother play. "I'll never be his little sister again, and he'll never be my big brother. Nothing will ever be the same again."

"That's what we said before I died," Shah Jehan said. "And centuries later, they'll be saying the same thing."

"Wait." Maera sat up as her mind reeled with questions. "You died in, what, 1947? Ammi was born thirty-two years after that." Maera felt her world tilt and spin.

The churail stared at Asad, chittering and giggling to himself. "You know what we churailain excel at?" Maera shook her head. "Seduction. I feel no shame in it. It's what we churailain do. Your naana would visit me over the years on our birthdays. He felt he had to, and I'd approach him in that form, my true form."

Maera shuddered, recalling her first meeting with her grandmother, the way she slithered across the ground, nails gouging the earth. The churail smiled a dreamy smile. "Oh, he was frightened. Terrified. Then, I would change myself to look like I would if I were his age."

The earth shifted beneath Maera again. The air ribboned in hazy waves; Maera felt like she were watching the world through an old television set. She could hear a buzzing around her, a hum that made her drowsy.

She was standing in her naana's backyard in Pakistan. A few feet ahead, a younger version of Naana stood before the greenhouse door, his fingers curled around the handle, peering in the way Maera had the first time she'd made contact. When he turned his head to the side, his eyes landed on Maera. She took a step back and gasped.

"He can't see you," the churail said, materializing next to her. "He's looking at her. At me."

A copy of the churail stood beside Maera, while another sat at the foot of a tree in Naana's backyard.

"Where have you brought me?" Maera whispered.

"A remnant of my memories," the churail said. "It's all I have anymore."

"You just relive them over and over again? God, that's depressing."

The churail smirked. "I know no other way to while away the time. While I sit here, another century goes by."

Maera looked on as an older Haroon approached the churail's memory-self, his hair receding, his temples dipped in gray. He knelt on the ground as the churail leaned against a tree, sobbing into her hands.

"Shah Jehan?" Haroon asked.

The churail glanced up at him with her blood-red eyes. "This is where Ma used to sit and pray for me. Under this very tree."

Haroon crept closer and sat down in front of the churail. He reached for her pale hands. "I'm—I'm so sorry. For everything. Everything."

Next to Maera, the churail chuckled to herself. "I knew I couldn't get him with fear. I had to use something else."

Maera bristled. "I thought you loved him."

The churail fixed her dead eyes on Maera. She was quaking with fear inside, but she kept her gaze locked on her grandmother.

"Churailain don't feel love."

Maera was sure she heard a tiny pang of regret in her voice.

Maera tore her gaze away to watch the scene unfolding before them. The churail had her hand outstretched, and she touched Haroon's cheek. His eyes softened as she drew him in for a kiss.

Maera looked away. "I don't need to see all this."

"You don't have to." The churail pointed her chin back at the greenhouse where the memory-churail held Haroon's hand and led him inside. The door swung shut behind them.

"Please do not tell me what happened next." Maera wrinkled her nose.

"You're old enough to know," the churail said. The memory rippled and dissolved into thin air, and Maera felt like a soft, dry blanket had been ripped off. They were back in the clearing, under the thunderous clouds.

"You raised my mom and aunt in here?" Maera asked with a sweeping gesture to indicate the greenhouse.

The churail clicked her tongue. Maera found the sound startlingly familiar to the one Ammi made when she wanted to say "no".

"I had them in here. Then, he took them away from me, raised them out there in his house with his brothers. He was mortified of what we'd created."

Maera rubbed the sweat forming at the back of her neck. She felt the dampness in the greenhouse closing in around her. "But my mom is fully human. I know she is."

"Some things are unexplainable." The churail smiled.

Somewhere in the trees, Asad was playing, swinging from limb to limb. Maera peered into the canopy but couldn't see him.

"You said churailain don't feel love, but you could have killed both Asad and my naana. Whatever part of you that's still human, that had two human daughters, that part of you still lives. All this time, he feared you, I feared you, you were here . . ."

"Waiting."

Maera spotted a trace of humanity in the churail's eyes, of the person the churail should have been if she hadn't died. Despite herself, Maera felt drawn to the churail, but the thought of their kinship made her queasy.

"You've been hurt in the past," Maera said. "But now my mom is hurting. There is a part of you that must know that." She picked up Asad's toys and pocketed the little animals. "It's time for Asad to come home."

The churail's face was set in stone. She rose to her full height, fingernails poised like claws. Maera jerked back instinctively.

"He can never leave. There are things you'll never understand. About life and death. About mortality. Humanity doesn't make you kind or gracious. It can turn you into a monster," she hissed.

Maera stared at the churail, willing herself not to blink. "I sacrificed myself to get my brother back."

The churail cackled and rose into the air. "You sacrificed yourself to see him again. Not take him back." The churail pointed toward the woods. "You may leave at any time. He cannot."

Maera backed away and ran into the trees, searching for Asad, but he was nowhere to be found.

She heard a giggle ahead, and she pressed further into the woods, following the sounds of creaking limbs as he jumped from one tree to the next. Then, Maera tripped on a fallen branch and stumbled.

The churail appeared in front of her, baring her fangs. "You don't know what you're doing."

"Give him back!" Maera yelled. "Asad belongs at home." The wind swirled around her; dead leaves flew up and hit her in the face. Maera picked herself up and ran to a tree ahead—she had spotted Asad at the top. She held out her arms. "Come down."

Asad looked down at her with a puzzled look on his face.

She pulled the wooden animals out of her pocket and held them up. "I have your toys here. Come down, and I'll let you play with them."

"But I'm having fun. Go away."

"We have to go home. Come on." A gust of wind barreled into Maera, and the toys fell from her hands, skittering off into the bushes. As Maera crawled around to pick them out of the dirt, Asad watched her from up in the tree.

"I don't want to go," he whined. He climbed farther into the tree, then swung on a vine and disappeared into the leaves.

"No!" Maera screamed. She darted around scanning the treetops, but Asad had disappeared.

Maera found her way back to the clearing. The churail had disappeared, but she could hear her murmuring in the wind. Then, white shrouds began to dot the trees around the clearing. Dozens of churailain slunk out of the woods and stood back to watch the wind whip around her. There were others, so many that Maera possibly couldn't count them all.

A scream lodged itself in her throat.

"Who are you?" Maera asked, shouting over the wind. They didn't utter a word; they just stared at her, their hands limp at their sides, twisted feet resting on the earth. Maera spun around, looked for something familiar, but she was in a strange part of the greenhouse. There was nowhere to go.

She took a seat on the stone conjured up by the churail and gripped the rock beneath her. "I want to go home," she begged. "Please, I want to go home."

Maera shut her eyes. She could sense the other churailain moving around her. Then, suddenly, the ground rippled under her feet, and the clearing restructured itself into the interior of a forest. When she finally opened her eyes, she found that she had somehow made it back to her backyard, but there was something terribly wrong.

# TWENTY-THREE

# THE FOREST

Maera couldn't make out her house in the dark.

All around her, dense clusters of peepal trees had thrust themselves out of the ground, their roots gnarled and ancient-looking. Maera struggled to breathe in the heavy, wet air.

"It's everywhere," Maera whispered as if the trees around her could hear. She took a step back, and her foot connected with something soft. Maera turned around, and her hand flew to her mouth.

Everyone was on the ground, lying in a semi-circle, arms out to their sides, eyes closed. Maera bent down to touch Ammi, whose leg she'd collided with when she stepped backward. She gingerly felt her face, and it was still warm. Next, Maera crawled over to inspect Aisha Khala, who lay in the same peaceful repose as Ammi. Sara and Jimmy were after that, lying close to each other, their hands touching.

Maera crept up to Rob, whose face looked troubled and eyebrows knitted. She checked to see if he was breathing—his breath tickled the side of her face as she bent over him, and his lips brushed her cheek. Maera sat back and touched the spot as she stared at the rest of them. She held her breath, willing herself not to cry.

Thunder roared overhead as heavy clouds crashed into one another and produced a torrent of green rain. It slithered down her face and made the others stir. Jimmy sat up first, glancing around at the others.

"I'm here." Maera's tears mingled with the slimy rain as it snaked under her collar.

Jimmy took hold of Sara and pulled her up into his arms. "I'm dreaming again," he said.

Maera crawled over to him. "This isn't a dream. It's spreading, and it's taking over everything."

Jimmy stared at Sara as raindrops plopped on her face. She shook herself awake and gasped. Maera helped her sit up, and Sara threw herself at Maera, giving her a fierce hug.

"You're alive!" Sara cried. "I'm so sorry. I'm sorry about everything I said to you."

Maera hugged her back. "You don't have to apologize for anything. Help me wake them." Sara inched her way to Rob and shook him hard.

With Sara out of earshot and the hiss of rain providing some cover, Maera turned back to Jimmy. He was sitting between the mothers, lifting their arms and watching them fall like dead branches back to the ground.

"One moment, we were here with our mothers, and the next, these trees separated us."

"Did you know?" Maera asked.

Jimmy looked pained for a moment. He shook his mother's shoulders; Aisha Khala groaned and turned on her side. Jimmy brushed sticky green strands of hair from her face.

"All this while, I thought it was because of her that I was able to enter, almost like she was giving me permission," Maera continued. "But she wasn't. You and I could have come and gone all along. It had a touch of our blood in it."

"And now it's all around us." Jimmy looked around him. "She's our grandmother, isn't she? We're her flesh and blood, which means all this is a part of us too." He blinked to get the green rain out of his eyes, avoiding the look Maera gave him. "I had a suspicion because the diary does not mention what happened to Shah Jehan after—after she died."

"We could have controlled it then." Maera gestured at the forest around her. "So, which one of us caused this to happen?"

Jimmy finally met her gaze. Ammi muttered in her sleep beside them.

"I understood why you did what you did, and I forgive you," Jimmy spoke in careful, deliberate tones. "I forgive you," he repeated. "Just as you would forgive me if I did the same."

Behind them, Sara had helped Rob sit up. He tried to wipe his face, but the green slime only spread everywhere.

Rob looked up at Maera and smiled at her. She stifled a sob as he pulled her into a hug. She was so surprised at the sudden gesture that by the time she remembered to hug him back, he'd already let go. He held her face in his hands, his eyes scanning her own. Then, he touched her shoulders and rubbed her arms, slathering the slime rain onto both of them.

"I'm not hurt," Maera said. "She let me go. She wouldn't let me take him. One second he was there in front of me, and the next, she took him away, and they disappeared."

She watched the disappointment surface on their faces when they realized Asad wasn't with her.

"You saw him," Rob said. "Did he—did he remember me?"

Maera bit her lip. The rain tasted like crushed leaves and bitter earth. "We didn't get to talk much."

Above them, the clouds crackled with static energy and let loose a low rumble.

"It's spreading like a virus," Sara said. "Our neighborhood is gone."

"I know why," Maera replied, while Jimmy busied himself helping the mothers, who were starting to regain consciousness and were struggling to sit up.

"I've made contact with my brother, but the churail won't let him go. If I don't overpower her, we will never get him back."

Jimmy looked at her. "This wasn't in the diary."

Maera sighed. "I can assure you that not all of our naana's secrets were in the diary. This jungle will spread and take over everything. We need to destroy her to make everything right again."

Jimmy frowned, but Maera put up a hand to stop his protests.

Ammi pushed herself to sit. She wiped the rain from her eyes and looked around. Aisha Khala rose next to her, identical expressions of horror on their faces as they took in the dense trees towering over them.

Ammi yelped when Maera crawled over to her. Maera glared at her, suddenly angry.

"Your mother did this."

The mothers blinked in unison.

"What? What are you talking about?" Aisha Khala asked.

Ammi's lip trembled. "She died giving birth to us."

"She was already dead."

The mothers gaped at her; Ammi breathed hard through her tears. She hugged herself and rocked back and forth. "I don't know what's happening."

"That greenhouse? There is a churail in there, and she's had Asad all this time. All these years."

"Stop it." Ammi wrung her hands. "Stop making up these stories. Please stop it." Ammi stared at Aisha Khala for help. "I—I don't know what to do."

The trees groaned and shook. Maera pulled the toy animals from her pocket and squeezed them, and the sharp edges pricked her palm. "One of these days, you'll have to wake up and face the tragedy unfolding around us. I'm tired of trying to stifle my pain and walk on eggshells around you. You have to listen to me now. We have to talk about The Past. And if we get through this, then someday, we'll have to talk about my future, too."

Ammi's lip trembled as she let out a heavy sob, but Maera finally had her attention.

"You can't be afraid anymore. Neither of us can. We don't have time left for that."

Ammi was silent, her tears leaving trails through the green slime on her cheeks.

"He's in here somewhere." Maera handed her the wooden animals; they clattered as they fell into her hands. Ammi turned them over and over and let out a soft whimper. The wooden figures dropped from her hands to the ground.

Aisha Khala swooped in and held Ammi in her arms while Maera picked the toys up and folded them back into her mother's palm.

"We have to get him back," Maera said.

Ammi glanced up at Maera with tired eyes. She nodded and let herself be helped to her feet by Sara and Aisha Khala. Rob took Maera's hand and helped her stand.

They turned back to the house—it had morphed into a different shape and now glittered between the trees. Maera took the lead, cutting through the foliage, shielding her face from the rain.

It wasn't her house anymore. The castle from the greenhouse stood in its place with its door wide open. Maera waited until the others assembled behind her, and then she stepped inside.

# TWENTY-FOUR

# THE HOUSE

Maera walked through a dark tunnel, guided by a hazy sepia light at the end. As she emerged into the light, she found herself in Naana's house in Pakistan. Behind her, she heard Ammi and Aisha Khala gasping.

"No, no, no," Ammi said, her voice rising. "I don't want this."

She turned to flee. Maera threw her arms around her and held her still. "I'm here," Maera said, whispering into Ammi's shoulder. "I'm with you."

Ammi hiccupped and held Maera close. "I don't know if I can do this."

"We don't have a choice."

Maera turned back to the courtyard. As she led Ammi in, Jimmy appeared beside her, wiping the rain from his cheeks, though Maera knew he was brushing away more than just raindrops. He held Aisha Khala's hand, who trembled at the scene unfolding before them.

Rob and Sara joined them, murmuring in surprise when the front door creaked opened on its own. Maera passed through the doorway and stared in wonder at what lay beyond.

Everything looked the same from when Maera last saw her grandfather's house. The building was still oblong, with an open-air courtyard in the center, lined with rooms. The first floor was shaded in darkness; a lone charpai sat facing the courtyard. This was where Naana used to sit and brood, smoking cigarette after cigarette, while the rest of the house went about their business.

Maera's feet slapped against the concrete as she approached the charpai. She thought she heard a distinctive creak, as if a body had just sat down in it. She looked up and counted the empty bedrooms on the second floor, their doors swinging in the wind. It was the same number of rooms.

"He's in here somewhere."

Maera turned back to the others, but they were transfixed, staring past her in terror. Then, from behind her, a sweet voice cried out.

"Ammi!"

Asad was sitting cross-legged on Naana's charpai.

The others were so still that Maera wondered if they had been somehow frozen in time.

Then, Rob strode past Maera, inching closer to Asad. "I don't believe this."

Maera could see the tears in the corner of his eye. She wanted to wipe them away, to touch his cheek, help him understand how strange, and yet normal, all of it was. But, instead, she slipped her hand into his.

"My son." Ammi began to sob. She approached him, opening her arms for him. Asad giggled and hopped off the charpai, throwing his arms around her neck and resting his head on her shoulder. He patted her back. "Don't cry, Ammi."

Aisha Khala bent down beside them, grief and horror on her face. "How?"

The churail floated out of the darkened recesses beyond the charpai and made her way to the mothers, who watched her approach with confused looks on their faces.

Rob drew in a sharp breath, and Maera squeezed his hand. "It's all right. They know her."

The churail stood before Ammi and Aisha Khala, who encircled Asad in a protective embrace.

"Do you remember me?"

At once, Ammi's face lit up. "I saw you once." She turned to Aisha Khala. "You never believed me when I told you I saw her in Abbu's greenhouse."

Aisha Khala stared at the churail's feet, a scowl on her face. The churail hesitated, then touched each of the mothers on the head. They rose together and stared back at the churail.

"Who are you?" Aisha Khala asked.

Before the churail had a chance to respond, the house shuddered. Someone was banging and rattling the door to the garden at the end of the courtyard. The group grew quiet, their eyes trained on the door as it shook again. Then, they heard an animal growl. The door rattled again, and its lower hinge broke off and fell to the ground.

The churail disappeared, but Maera heard a voice inside her head. "I told you it's no use," it said. "I'm not the only one who needs him."

Maera turned back to the others. "We have to get out of here."

Ammi stared at the charpai. "Where did she go?"

"This way," Maera yelled and took hold of Asad's hand, pulling him along as the rest of them followed close behind.

A roar echoed behind them. Sara stopped to look and screamed, but Maera continued to race ahead through the outer courtyard, Asad's soft hand in hers. Her palm was slick with sweat, and she felt his fingers slipping from her grip.

"Come on!"

They flung themselves out of the castle and sprinted through the mess of vines and trees before them.

The churail suddenly reappeared, and Maera skidded to a halt. Rubble from the castle skittered around her feet.

"You can't have him," Maera gasped. She pushed Asad behind her to shield him. "He's coming home."

"I can't have him anymore," the churail repeated and smirked. "But you didn't ask how he felt about it."

Behind them, the castle shivered as deep cracks tore through its surface. Chunks of stone broke away and thundered to the ground. A deep rumbling shook the earth, and Maera felt her legs give out underneath her. She fell to the ground along with the others behind her.

Jimmy crawled on his knees and elbows to Maera and pulled her up. They looked back at the castle as a monster ripped through the entrance: a brown beast with pulsing blue veins snaking across its skin. It didn't have a nose, just a gaping mouth filled with rows of sharp teeth. It glared at the rest of them, then turned its attention to Maera, who held Asad close to her on one side and Jimmy on the other.

The churail floated up and called out to them, "Children, meet your grandfather."

She swept her hand up to the sky. The monster howled as the walls of the castle warped and shattered. Shards of stone and glass fell like slivers of rain around them.

# TWENTY-FIVE

# THE CHASE

Maera's ears were ringing, and her eyes stung. When the smoke cleared, Maera leaned over Asad. He was lying on his back with a look of shock on his face; he had bits of stone sprinkled in his hair, but he was unhurt. Maera brushed the debris and pulled him up, and cradled him in her arms. Asad looked around in alarm, his chest rising and falling in rapid bursts like a terrified little bird. It was the first time she'd ever seen a look of fear on his face.

The beast strode above the broken remains of the castle. It swiveled its great head, searching for Maera and Asad, tearing trees out of the ground and hurling them. Maera picked Asad up in her arms and stumbled to the nearest tree. He was still listless and confused as she set him down beside her.

The monster watched with bleary eyes as the others managed to get on their feet and brush the dust off their clothes. The beast ignored them, wagging its head before it turned in the direction of Maera. Maera pulled Asad after her and hid behind the tree.

She peeked between the bushes to get a glimpse of what used to be her neighborhood—it was unrecognizable.

The houses had aged, covered in layers of moss. Thick vines burst through their windows. The greenhouse jungle was all around them now, no longer bound by the glass walls, no longer bound by anything.

Maera spotted Sara pulling Jimmy up and hugging him. At first, his hands were limp at his sides, and then he put his arms around her.

"Rob," Maera whispered.

Rob turned his head and squinted in her general direction. She waved until she caught his eye and put a finger to her lips. Above them, the monster growled and uprooted a tree. Rob helped Ammi and Aisha Khala to their feet and led them in the direction of Maera's hiding place, but they were walking too fast, and they missed her. Rob blinked the dust out of his eyes and scanned the area for her.

"I'm here," Maera whispered and waved at him again. The beast had its back turned; it was busy swiping at vines, ripping them into shreds.

"Rob," Maera called out louder.

Both Rob and the beast whipped around at the same time. Maera hid behind the tree and reached for Asad, but he was no longer there. Something grabbed Maera's shoulder, and she screamed. She turned around to punch the thing, but it was only Rob with the rest of her family crowding behind him.

"He's gone." They couldn't hear Maera's words over the monster's roar. It reared its head and bounded toward them, flattening bushes as it barreled toward them.

She turned to Jimmy. "Keep our moms safe." Jimmy nodded in agreement. He darted back for the mothers.

"I'm coming with you," Sara said, giving Maera an apologetic look.

"Do what you have to do."

Only Maera and Rob were left. A gust of humid air blew in their faces, and the ground shook. A broken tree crashed into the ones nearest them, just a few feet away. There was a low growl above them. The beast's face peered down at them from above the canopy. Maera screamed as Rob swept in and hugged her, using his body as a shield, their hearts thumping in unison.

Over Rob's shoulder, she saw the beast glare at her and emit a low grumble. She stared back at it, but it didn't move to attack her. Instead, its eyes swept the forest floor searching for Asad, and it mumbled something that sounded like speech. Maera recalled her grandfather's face—his empty eyes—and found the memory startlingly similar to the monster's face above her.

"What happened to you?" she whispered. The beast blinked and then swiped at the trees next to her, pulling them up by their roots.

Rob drew her away from the carnage. "I think I know where he may have gone," he said. "The only place here in our neighborhood that is familiar to him. I'm going to find him."

"You can't leave," Maera said.

Rob's lips were close to Maera's ear. "Do you remember what I said to you right before your parents closed the door on me forever?"

Maera realized with a jolt that she'd forgotten he'd ever said anything to her at all. All this time, she had only remembered his forlorn face staring back at her, but as her memory readjusted, she saw his lips move.

"I said I'd always be there for you. And I wasn't." Rob held her for a brief moment and then let go. "Trust me."

He stepped away from Maera, waving his arms at the monster. "Come on!"

The monster growled and reached for Rob, who dodged its massive fingers and ran into the woods, his footsteps muffled by a thick carpet of moss.

# TWENTY-SIX

# THE RESTORATION

Maera ran after them but soon snagged her foot on a vine and fell headlong on the mossy ground, her forehead crashing against a rock. She rolled onto her back and blinked back the sudden tears, only to find that her vision was blurred by a crack in the lens of her glasses. The commotion drew Sara and Jimmy from deep inside the woods.

"Are you okay?" Jimmy asked while Maera pushed up from the ground and got to her feet.

"We can't find them," Sara said. "I don't know where they've gone."

"They have to be around here somewhere." Maera looked around wildly—the trees seemed to be closing in on them.

"That thing is probably headed for Rob's house. I have to go save him."

Maera sprinted through the trees until she was at Rob's front door, only to find that a thick trunk had broken it in half. She crawled through the bottom half of the door and staggered into the living room.

Rob's parents lay motionless on the couch: green vines had wrapped themselves around their bodies, making them look like mummies. A churail stood over them, studying their terrified faces.

"Don't," Maera said. The churail swiveled to face Maera. "It wasn't their fault."

The churail eyed Maera for a moment, then she straightened up and folded her hands in front of her. She watched Maera as she backed away.

Maera ran in and out of rooms, but Rob was nowhere to be found. Then, bits of the roof began to rain down upon her. She covered her head as she looked up to find the beast peeking into the house from where the top of the house used to be. It growled when it saw Maera, then stomped away.

Maera crawled back out of Rob's house and sank to the ground. The air was thick with dust. She coughed, imagining it trickling down her throat and coating her lungs. It wouldn't be long before they'd all suffocate or be trapped by the snake-like vines constantly threatening to take hold of them.

Maera covered her face with her hands and let the tears overwhelm her. She couldn't remember the last time she'd cried this much, but now she let everything out, and her sobbing ricocheted against the unforgiving forest.

Maera didn't have to look to know the churail had materialized before her; she had a green aura around her. Maera took in the churail's grim face.

"Why do you cry?"

"Everything's lost. Asad will never grow up. He'll never get to be an adult; he won't be my older brother again. My whole world is destroyed. I've lost Rob . . ." Maera began to cry again.

The churail sighed. "Think about your brother. Think about him."

Maera wiped her tears, leaving green streaks on her face. "I have. Every single day since he disappeared."

The churail grimaced and gave her an exasperated look. "Think about who he was before he left you."

Maera slipped off her broken glasses and rubbed her eyes. "He was a rambunctious kid. So full of energy. He could never sit still; he'd run from one end of the house to the other, back and forth. He and Rob—" Maera stopped, overwhelmed by the memories bursting forth from a treasure chest inside her. She slipped her glasses back on and stood to face the churail. "Why are you trying to help me?"

The churail looked into the distance. "We aren't wholly evil," she mused. "When you've lost almost everything, what do you hold onto?"

"Come with me," Maera said. "Help me defeat him."

The churail shook her head. "There is no defeating him." She put up a hand to silence her. "I will come with you. You go ahead, and I'll follow."

Maera plunged through the forest with the churail gliding alongside her. Even in the changing landscape, Maera knew where to go. She headed past the houses on her street to the end of the cul-de-sac. There used to be a small natural woodland there that was now overrun by the jungle. She parted the foliage to reveal an overgrown trail that led to a playground where Rob and Asad used to play. Ammi never knew about this secret hideout, and she would always lose her mind trying to figure out where he'd gone. It was derelict now, the slide was cracked in half, and the swings were only partially hanging from the chains, making eerie creaking sounds in the wind. Maera wiped the sweat off her brow. She walked through the playground to reach the edge of the forest where a small pond used to lie.

When she was younger, Maera was fascinated by how clean and shiny the pond looked, though she and Asad had been forbidden from swimming in it. It was now covered in a green slimy layer, dotted with lily pads, like the pond Maera found in the greenhouse. At the water's edge sat Asad with his feet dipped in the water. Rob sat next to him, gazing at his old friend. Asad said something and kicked his feet; he laughed when the water splashed onto them.

Maera took a few cautious steps forward but stopped when she spotted the beast. It was about a hundred feet away but seemed much closer because of its size. It sat on its haunches, head hanging low as it watched Asad and Rob.

A twig snapped near Maera, and she flinched. As she did, bits of the green slime, now dried and cracked, flaked off her arms.

Jimmy and Sara joined her. They peeked out from behind a tree together.

"What do we do now?" Sara asked. "Nothing's happening. It's almost too peaceful."

Maera looked up at the churail. "We all lost someone important to us. Surely you understand that now. We're fighting for him," Maera said. "All of us are."

"I can't help you," the churail said.

"I know," Maera said. "'There are things I just won't understand.'"

The churail turned her attention back to the pond and smiled. From the other side of the pond, Ammi stepped out of the woods and approached the boys, her eyes focused. The beast swung its head in Ammi's direction and emitted a low growl, but Ammi neither heard nor saw it.

Behind her, Aisha Khala watched her sister approach her child; she gripped a tree for support. The beast stood up to its full height and lumbered forward, but again, Ammi noticed nothing.

"We have to do something," Maera said. "He'll hurt her."

"No," Jimmy said.

Maera looked at him. "What did you say?"

Jimmy held out a wavering hand. "Please don't do anything. He is harmless."

"He tried to attack us," Maera said, her impatience constricting her chest and threatening to cut off her air. Her fists shook as she turned to him. "Just look at him. He's a monster."

She was met with impassive faces in reply.

The beast watched Ammi with its red, watery eyes. She was just a few feet from Asad, and she held her arms out in front of her, ready to snatch him up. The beast growled.

"If you all won't do anything, then I will," Maera stepped out of the wood. Sara grabbed her arm to stop her.

"Listen to Jimmy," she said with a look imploring her to understand.

Maera yanked herself away. "That thing is going to kill us all just to get Asad back."

"He hasn't done anything to hurt us," Jimmy said.

Maera's mouth hung open. "Are you—are you on his side?"

The churail floated to Jimmy and placed a hand on his shoulder.

Jimmy's lip trembled. "Our naana was flawed, but that monster isn't him. I understand it now. This is who he thought he was in life." Jimmy glanced at the churail. "He left that part of himself to you, didn't he?"

The churail nodded. "That was our agreement. If he took my babies away, he needed to give me something in return when he died."

"He was the living embodiment of that." Maera pointed in its direction. "He was a living, breathing monster to our mothers. And you're standing up for him."

"He was trying to protect them," Sara said. "He was afraid. It doesn't mean he did the right thing." Sara looked up at the churail, who placed a gentle hand on top of her head.

"And that makes him an honorable man?"

"Who among us isn't flawed?" Jimmy said.

A scream rose inside Maera. "I should've known all along that the only one who cares about my family is me."

Maera charged out into the clearing as the monster made to reach for Ammi. The earth trembled, and Ammi stumbled back. That's when she noticed the creature and screamed. Rob scrambled to his feet as Maera ran toward her mother, but it was too late.

The monster scooped Ammi and Aisha Khala into his palms and brought them up to his face.

"He's hurting them!" Maera cried, pulling Asad up. She looked back at the churail. "Do something!"

Sara, Jimmy, and the churail were staring at the beast with rapt attention.

"Help us!" Maera shouted, but only Rob seemed to hear her. He drew closer, and Maera buried her face in his chest.

"You have to see this," Rob said, lifting her chin with his finger so that their eyes met.

"I can't." Maera's tears blurred Rob's features into a hazy puddle. "He's going to kill them."

"No. You have to look." He pushed Maera in front of him to see.

Through her broken glasses, Maera could make out the mothers standing on the beast's outstretched hands. Its red eyes darted between them, and as it exhaled, its breath ruffled their clothes and hair. Then, finally, it murmured something that only the sisters could hear.

Ammi and Aisha Khala clasped hands, and Ammi held up her free hand to caress the beast's chin. Aisha Khala stretched her hand out as well, and the beast lowered its great head for them. They rubbed its bumpy skin. The beast raised its head as they spoke to him quietly.

It hit Maera that the words weren't for her or the others to hear; they'd spent decades distilling the unsaid words and were finally letting them come to the surface. Churailain popped up around them, some seated in the branches, others with their feet planted on the ground, all of them entranced by the monster.

Maera looked at Asad, who clung to her side with a placid expression on his face. He let Maera's hand drop. "No," she said and took his hand and squeezed it. Though he was so close to her, she felt further from him than she had ever felt before. He looked at the churail, slipped his hand from Maera's, and began walking away. Maera wanted to scoop him up in her arms again, but this time, Maera knew she couldn't fight to keep him. He left them, as he did so many years ago.

Maera felt her chest unknot—this was the sacrifice the churail had asked of her. As he retreated into the distance, Maera exhaled deeply after what felt like so many years of holding her breath.

Asad took the churail's hand, and soon they joined the beast. It lowered its hand to the ground, letting Ammi and Aisha Khala step off and find their footing on the mossy floor below.

As the churail and Asad neared, Ammi and Aisha Khala stared at her wide-eyed, looking perplexed.

"Ammi!" Asad hugged her mother, flashing a dimpled smile.

"My darlings." The churail drew the mothers into a hug. "I never had a chance to say goodbye to you. Now I can." She took each of their faces in her hands, kissed them on the forehead, then stepped away to look up at the beast. "It's time we go. You've caused enough trouble for today." The beast snorted in response.

Maera and the others assembled around the mothers. Jimmy put a comforting arm around Maera. "I think I understand it now," Maera said to him. "This is what he wanted us to do. Meet Shah Jehan and set them both free."

Jimmy squeezed her shoulder. "And set our mothers free, too."

They watched as the churail held her hand out to Asad. "Come along now," she said to him.

Asad peeled himself away from Ammi to take the churail's hand once again. Maera didn't move to stop him and wasn't surprised when her mother didn't either. They watched Asad and the churail disappear into the woods.

The beast lingered for a moment with his daughters, then turned his head away and ambled into the trees.

# TWENTY-SEVEN

# THE PAST

Back at Maera's backyard, a fierce wind picked up, whipping everyone's hair and clothes against their bodies. Then, before their shocked eyes, the greenhouse repaired itself. Peepal trees broke free from the earth and were sucked back into the greenhouse. The green dust in the air and the moss coating the ground followed. Vines were ripped from the houses, hurtling past them to return to their jungle. Maera hugged Ammi while Jimmy held Aisha Khala's hand as the group watched the greenhouse pull back all of its destructive energy.

Soon enough, the sun broke through the clouds and shone brightly, and birds began to chirp.

"Rob?" A voice called out from his backyard. "Where'd you go, buddy?" his dad asked.

"Thank goodness they're okay," Maera said as Rob looked in the direction of his house.

"What was wrong with them in the first place?"

Maera grinned and nudged him toward his backyard.

He touched her hand. "I'll—I'll call you," he said.

"Are you asking for my number?" Maera asked. She raised her chin at the loose planks in the backyard fence. "I prefer the element of surprise."

Rob backed away, waving at the rest of them. He slipped into his backyard and, when he'd safely returned to his house, Maera turned to face the greenhouse. Jimmy stood in the doorway, peering in.

"I'm sorry," she said. "For not believing you. I'm sorry I was such a brat to deal with."

"You wanted your family back together again," Jimmy said as he watched Ammi embrace Aisha Khala. "I don't blame you."

"I'm sorry you can't have your dad back."

"I'm sorry you can't have Asad back."

"I guess we'll just have to live with it then."

"I guess." Jimmy smiled. "We're together in this at least."

Sara curled her fingers into Jimmy's when Maera noticed that Jimmy held the diary in his other hand. He looked away nervously when he realized she'd spotted it.

"That one last bit of paper," Maera said. "I want to see it now."

Jimmy opened the diary and handed her the newspaper clipping. They unfolded it to read it together, Sara reading over Jimmy's shoulder. Maera was relieved that it was in English, ripped from an Indian newspaper. It was about what she'd learned recently from Shah Jehan: the story of how Partition had affected her grandparents' hometown, how the country she thought she knew had sprung forth from the blood and ruin of another.

"Did you know about this?" Maera asked him. Jimmy frowned. "No one ever wants to talk about it. Did you?"

Sara shook her head. "Our history is kept away from us because we were born here. I had no idea all of this happened. But now that I do, I'm going to talk to my mom about it," she said.

Maera let go of the clipping. "The Past doesn't feel like The Past; it's part of the present now." She smiled at Jimmy as he folded it and placed it back between the pages of the diary. "You can keep the diary," she said, looking back at Ammi and Aisha Khala heading into the house together. "I think I've already got what I need."

Jimmy and Sara left Maera in the backyard and followed after the mothers, still holding hands.

Maera touched the greenhouse door. It felt lifeless: the structure didn't throb; there were no gusts of wind animating the greenery.

"Thank you," Maera whispered. She leaned against the door for a while before turning toward the house.

# EPILOGUE

On the last day of summer, Ammi walked into Maera's room wearing a flowery shalwar kameez, a white sun hat, and oversized gardening gloves.

"Come on," she said. "You promised you'd help me."

Maera groaned and rolled over. "I'll be out in ten minutes."

Ammi was already toiling away inside the greenhouse by the time Maera stepped outside. The sun was intense, high in the sky, and Maera felt like she were baking in her T-shirt and jeans.

She stood in the doorway and watched. Ammi had set up planters filled with herbs along the periphery—cilantro and mint, with a bit of basil thrown in for her favorite lemonade. In the center, she was growing more challenging plants: root vegetables and lettuce, interlaced by vines of tomatoes and grapes. In the back of the greenhouse stood an optimistic-looking peepal tree. Ammi was fussing with the herbs when Maera entered.

"You think it'll survive out here in not-Pakistan?" Maera asked, eyeing the tree.

"It survived the travel," Ammi said and frowned. "I'm only good at growing the easier stuff. I'll really need your help with the rest before you head off to college," she said. "Can I have you for at least one more year?"

"That's what I'm here for." Maera grinned at Ammi. She picked up a watering can and shook to see how much water was left. "I don't know how that tree is going to survive in Virginia."

Ammi tittered, all girlish and light on her feet. She joined Maera to scrutinize the peepal tree.

"You think this greenhouse will ever return to the way it was?" Maera asked.

"I don't know," Ammi said. "But I'm all right with the way things are now."

She let out a soft sigh, and a few of the peepal leaves shook.

"Me too," Maera said. She smiled at the presence of family around her. Somehow, in some way, Maera knew they were all with her in Shah Jehan's greenhouse. Maera made a promise to herself that she'd tend to their roots for as long as she lived.

Maera patted the trunk of the peepal tree, and its leaves rustled in response. Then, she headed back to help Ammi fuss over her herbs.

# AUTHOR'S NOTE

I've always felt that Pakistani people, or even hyphenated diaspora members such as myself, have a complicated relationship with history. My family doesn't have an illustrated family tree hanging on the wall in their living room. I don't know who my great-grandparents were; I never spent time with my own grandparents since they lived in Pakistan. Whatever I'd ever learned about the Indian subcontinent was what my high school history books wanted to include. And they didn't include much.

When you grow up in America, you normalize your ancestral history as a series of footnotes in the larger history of the Western world.

Many years ago in high school, one of these brief historical asides fascinated me. I learned that in the year 1947, the Indian subcontinent spiraled into violence and bloodshed following a mass migration of Muslims and Hindus crossing a border between what is now present-day India and Pakistan. People had to involuntarily leave their country for a different one because of their religion. And the road to their new homes was paved with violence.

Millions on both sides were hurt, killed, or kidnapped as they made their way—often on foot—to their new country. It sounds dystopian, but it happened.

I came home and asked my mother about Partition. She told me that my grandparents both lived through it. They were married as teenagers; my grandmother was made to dress as a boy to protect her from abduction or assault. This was explained to me as matter-of-fact. The first place they arrived in Pakistan was Hyderabad in the province of Sindh. My grandparents claimed it as the place they'd build their new home where eventually my mother was born.

My head was spinning. I wanted to research every single place my mother told me about that day. I didn't know what Sindh was or where to locate Hyderabad on a map of Pakistan. But what struck me was if I hadn't directly asked my mother, she'd never have volunteered any of that information. And I know that it would have been the same for her—she likely had to ask her parents to tell her about Partition because they wouldn't have volunteered it either.

Sometime later, I was learning about World War II in my World History class. By now, I knew that India used to be a colony of the British Empire (the repercussions of which weren't expanded on), so I casually asked my father about it. He mentioned he had an uncle who fought in the war for the British Empire and survived. He came home a hero; my father spoke proudly of the times he'd met him. Again, I couldn't believe what I was hearing. All I knew about World War II was the narrative dominated by white faces that I saw on film and television and what I read in my history books about the European Allies. I knew nothing about the colonized people who had to fight on behalf of the British while protesting their independence from their colonizer at the same time. And again, if I hadn't asked my father directly, I'd never know about it.

I mention in the book that brown people are haunted. Growing up, I heard more stories about jinns and churails coming for us if we stayed out late at night than I did about my ancestors. And I know now why my parents never sat down to regale us with tales about their ancestors—those tales were likely unhappy and violent. In a way, stories about jinns and churails felt as if they were an explanation without going into history. Perhaps when you're a colonized people, it's not a history you want to remember.

But who shaped our history and made it so complicated for us?

When I set out to write *House of Glass Hearts*, this was the question I wanted to answer. I wanted to write about the brutal subjugation of the Indian subcontinent when the British Empire decided to colonize it, whose repercussions are still being felt today. India never got to experience an industrial revolution. British colonization disenfranchised the subcontinent economically, culturally—and given the current-day geopolitical conundrum we're in—sociopolitically.

Am I the best person to write this story? As a first-generation American with Pakistani immigrant parents whose own parents were Indian immigrants, I own that my identity is complicated. So, I've rooted the story in my own family's history. My grandparents are long gone, but I've added historical touches from what I was able to learn from my parents—the character Shah Jehan, who also has to dress as a boy to migrate, is named after my grandmother. Kanpur/Cawnpore in Uttar Pradesh is where my grandparents grew up before they had to leave India. I've also turned to historians such as Yasmin Khan and read Partition literature from Khushwant Singh to ground the story with historical facts. And just for fun, I watched a ton of Bombay Talkies films from the 1940s to visualize how pre-Partition India might have looked, sounded, dressed, and loved, and slowly became an Ashok Kumar stan in the process.

History is often a series of causalities. There are enormous implications for what colonization did to my ancestors and their Hindu and Sikh neighbors and brethren. And so, perhaps within these pages is a silent plea that instead of taking sides against our own people, our neighbors across the border, we should recognize and work to heal from the horrors of imperialism together.

**Further reading:**

Karnad, Raghu. *Farthest Field: An Indian Story of the Second World War*. W. W. Norton & Company, 2015

Khan, Yasmin. *The Raj at War: A People's History of India's Second World War*. Vintage, 2016

Khan, Yasmin. *The Great Partition: The Making of India and Pakistan*. Yale University Press, 2008

Mukerjee, Madhusree. *Churchill's Secret War: The British Empire and the Ravaging of India during World War II*. Basic Books, 2010

Raghavan, Srinath. *India's War: World War II and the Making of Modern South Asia*. Basic Books, 2016

Singh, Khushwant. *Train to Pakistan*. Grove Press, 1994

Singh, Khushwant, Bhisham Sahni, Saadat Hasan Manto. *Memories of Madness: Stories of 1947*. Penguin Global, 2003

Stewart, Frank Henderson, ed. *Crossing Over: Partition Literature from India, Pakistan, and Bangladesh*. University of Hawaii Press, 2007

CPSIA information can be obtained
at www.ICGtesting.com
Printed in the USA
BVHW071934141021
618959BV00004B/231